Sherlock Holmes

And

The Escape Artist

Fred Thursfield

Paperback ISBN 978-1-78092-592-9
ePub ISBN 978-1-78092-593-6
PDF ISBN 978-1-78092-594-3

Published in the UK by MX Publishing
335 Princess Park Manor, Royal Drive, London, N11 3GX
www.mxpublishing.com
Cover design by www.staunch.com

Prologue

Do Spirits Return?
Harry Houdini says No and Proves It

Quoted from a promotional hand bill posted at the Lyceum theatre London

---

Harry Houdini was born as Erik Weisz in Budapest, Austria-Hungary, on March 24, 1874. His parents were Rabbi Mayer Sámuel Weisz, and Cecília Weisz (née Steiner). Houdini was one of seven children. Weisz arrived in the United States on July 3, 1878, sailing on the SS *Fresia* with his mother (who was pregnant) and his four brothers. The family changed the Hungarian spelling of their German surname to Weiss (the German spelling) and Erik's name was changed to Ehrich. Friends called him "Ehrie" or "Harry".

They first lived in Appleton, Wisconsin, where his father served as Rabbi of the Zion Reform Jewish Congregation. From 1907 on, Houdini would claim in interviews to have been born in Appleton, which was not true. According to the 1880 census, the family lived on Appleton Street. On June 6, 1882, Rabbi Weiss became an American citizen. Losing his tenure at Zion in 1887, Rabbi Weiss moved with Ehrich to New York City. They lived in a boarding house on East 79th Street. They were joined by the rest of the family once Rabbi Weiss found permanent housing.

As a child, Ehrich Weiss took several jobs, making his public début as a 9-year-old trapeze artist, calling himself "Ehrich, the Prince of the Air". He was also a champion cross country runner in his youth. When Weiss became a professional magician he began calling himself "Harry Houdini" because he was heavily influenced by the French magician Jean Eugène Robert-Houdini, and his friend Jack Hayman told him, erroneously, that in French, adding an "i" to Houdin would mean "like Houdin", the great magician. In later life, Houdini would claim that the first part of his new name, Harry, was homage to Harry Kellar, whom Houdini admired.

Until the success of his first act, Houdini had resorted to posing as a "spirit medium", gathering information from cemeteries and town clerks before shows to make his "messages" more convincing. In the 1920s, Harry became interested in the occult, specifically in debunking mediums and psychics. His training in magic helped him expose frauds that scientists and academics could not. He chronicled his time investigating the occult in his book, *A Magician among the Spirits*.

Houdini began his magic career in 1891. At the outset, he had little success. He performed in dime museums and sideshows, and even doubled as "The Wild Man" at a circus. Houdini focused initially on traditional card tricks. At one point, he billed himself as the "King of Cards". But he soon began experimenting with escape acts.

In 1893, while performing with his brother "Dash" (Theodore) at Coney Island as "The Brothers Houdini", Harry met a fellow performer Wilhelmina Beatrice (Bess) Rahner. Though Bess was initially courted by Dash, she and Houdini married in 1894, with Bess replacing Dash in the act, which became known as "The Houdini's." For the rest of Houdini's performing career, Bess would work as his stage assistant.

Houdini's big break came in 1899 when he met manager Martin Beck in rural Woodstock, Illinois. Impressed by Houdini's handcuffs act, Beck advised him to concentrate on escape acts and booked him on the Orpheum vaudeville circuit. Within months, he was performing at the top vaudeville houses in the country. In 1900, Beck arranged for Houdini to tour Europe. After some days of unsuccessful interviews in London, Houdini managed to interest Dundas Slater, then manager of the Alhambra Theatre. He gave a demonstration of escape from handcuffs at Scotland Yard, and succeeded in baffling the police so effectively that he was booked at the Alhambra for six months.

On January 7th, 1918 Houdini for the first time performed his "Vanishing Elephant" illusion at New York's Hippodrome Theater. The Hippodrome features the world's largest stage as well as a troupe of trained elephants.

The illusion called for only a huge cabinet, an elephant, and a team of twelve, strong men. Houdini began with a cabinet, he described as "about eight feet square, twenty six inches off the floor." All parts of the cabinets where shown to the audience and the elephant was walked inside. Once inside the cabinet, the doors and curtains were closed. Once reopened, the cabinet was empty, the elephant vanished.

Sherlock Holmes

And

The Escape Artist

As related from the personal notes of Mary N. Watson

London, 1922

Chapter 1

156 East
Forsyth Street,
New York City

Dear Mary

It seems like such a very long time since Peter and I visited with you while he and I were on holiday in London and the three of us together took in all the popular tourist sites and destinations there. I feel, and Peter agrees with me that it is time you had a change of scenery so we would like it very much if you make the crossing from England for a vacation and come to stay with us in New York City.

This would be a wonderful opportunity for us both to catch up on events in each other's lives, visit book shops together in the morning such as Saint Mark's Bookshop on 3rd Avenue, and Waldenbooks on Lexington Avenue, in the afternoon have lunch then after visit the many art galleries in Greenwich Village. In the evenings let Peter and I accompany you to some of the night time attractions that this city is famous for.

I thought that while you were staying with us here you may be interested in seeing some of the evening shows that are currently playing on Broadway. There is The Czarina at the Empire Theatre…Mr. Faust at the Province Town Play House and the most popular entertainer Harry Houdini the escape artist, and illusionist performing nightly at the Hippodrome.

I have read articles in the news papers reporting that Mr. Houdini can escape from any type of manufactured restraint or enclosure and that he has caused a full sized elephant to apparently just disappear from the stage to the awe and amazement of the audience attending.

Anticipating your acceptance I have already sent Peter along to the White Star Line ticket office in lower Broadway to inquire about all the necessary travel arrangements concerning your pending voyage.

I am including with this letter to you the information he was provided with for their flag ship the RMS Majestic which sails from the port of Southampton bound for New York City. Enclosed are passenger fares, available cabins on board as well as the ship's departure dates and times.

As well there is the Majestic's breakfast, luncheon and dinner menu selections and a full itinerary of daily activities for the passengers to avail themselves of during the crossing. We both look forward to seeing you very soon.

Warmly

Alice

126 Hill House Road,
London

Dear Alice

Yes with the somewhat worrying events involving my writer friend in Gravesend now happily resolved I agree that I am certainly due for a change and would love to come to New York City and spend time with my cousin and her husband. So my thanks to you both in extending a most warm and wonderful invitation and also for providing me with the necessary information for my voyage.

Shortly after posting this letter to you I will be making my way to the White Star Lines West-End ticket office located on Cockspur Street in Westminster (London) to book passage on the ship you have recommended in your letter to me.

If I can persuade a close friend of mine who is presently residing at Avignon in the South of France and has admired Mr. Houdini's well known escape artistry for some time to accompany me on the crossing could he please be included in our plans?

Yours

Mary

p.s. When I have finalized my travel arrangements and I have found someone to watch the house while I am away I will cable a telegram to you letting you know my departure date and time from the port of Southampton and also as to whether or not my friend will be accompanying me.

Mary.

While I was at the ticket office booking passage to cross the Atlantic Ocean I inquired about the ship that Alice had suggested in her letter to me. The RMS Majestic (working what the White Star Line calls the North Atlantic run) I was informed by the ticket agent it is the biggest ocean liner in their fleet with an impressive length of 956 feet from the bow to the stern and a beam (or width mid ship) of 100.1 feet.

Deciding this was the ship I wanted to be on to cross the Atlantic certainly I (and hopefully my traveling companion) along with 2,145 other passengers would be aboard as the Majestic continued the second leg of its maiden voyage sailing under its recently rechristened White Star Line name, and new British maritime registry (In 1922). A journey which had started from the port of Cherbourg France to Southampton England then finally on to New York City in America

After purchasing my ticket but before leaving to return home and pack I took some time to pause and admire the passenger lines collection of official standard 8 x 10 inch framed black and white company photographs depicting their ships that were accompanied by large and certainly bright and colourful advertisement posters each promoting the pleasures of ocean travel that collectively were tastefully displayed on the walls of the ticket office.

Most of the pictures and posters displayed were of the Majestic (but as well a few of the other passenger ships in their fleet) all set in different voyage settings and stationary views. The pictures and posters I saw that morning did not begin to do the Majestic any real justice as to when I witnessed for the time the gigantic liner (until that moment it had only been a name printed on my ticket) securely moored to the dock as I was exiting the vehicle that had brought me to my place of departure.

Southampton England by: Miss Sarah Cooper

Set on the coast of Hampshire, South of Winchester, this is a place that abounds with a fascinating heritage. The Romans had established it as a sea port approximately 2,000 years ago. This is the port from which the ill fated Titanic had set sail on her maiden voyage in 1912.

Even though the place was affected during the First World War, Southampton has grown sturdy with huge docks built for the shipping and passenger industry. The core of the modern city is now based around the City Centre.

As I was making my way along the busy, lively and well travelled wooden pier approaching the ship that would soon take me to New York City all the while passing stevedores and cargo handlers proceeding past me in both directions each going about with their heavy task I stopped, set my luggage down beside me...turned to my left for a minute or so to face, take in and fully appreciate the grand scale of the liner I was about to sail on.

With what was now grandly presented in front of me...like some great ocean going panorama sitting on the water of the morning sun lit harbour...I let my eyes travel from about the port hole horizontally lined mid section of the ship, smartly coated in the White Star livery (dove white, White Star "Buff" funnels, teal stripe and red cross markings, standard terra-cotta red keel) first far right to the bow...then travel slowly left again along the mid section of the ship back the long distance from the bow to finish at the stern.

Then I looked directly up from the side...first to the large open boarding hatch where the white canvas covered passenger gang way (already in use) was connected at a gentle angle from the pier to the side of the ship...then to the promenade deck (just one deck above) to where I could see passengers moving about who were already on board.

Then taking in the life boat deck as well the passenger cabin decks above it until my gaze ended with the command bridge to my right then just behind it was another set of life boats hanging in their davits and to their left the three in line large and tall guy wire supported active ships funnels (also coated in White Star livery) 30 feet in diameter and each with a reach of 184 feet above keel that defined the total height (bottom to top) of the ocean liner.

Just above and over the three large funnels was the Majestic's extensive radio antenna's which ran the length of the ship and were suspended between two tall guy wire braced masts…one mast located at the bow and the other at the stern of the liner.

After having my ticket and passage confirmed against the Majestic's passenger manifest by a smartly uniformed boarding officer…I proceeded (along with other passengers) on to the ship where I was in turn met and dutifully escorted (along with my carry on luggage) to my reserved cabin (being one of the 705 tourist class cabins available) by a helpful steward where…after I had comfortably settled in and become acquainted with my on board accommodations…I then unpacked and put away my clothing and toiletries.

When finished I left my compartment and made my way along the length of the warm incandescent lit interior passage way of the vessel then stepped from the inside through an open passenger hatch to the sunlit outside.

While walking along the bustling right promenade deck, passing chatting passengers gathered along the rail and others strolling by I purposefully made my way to the aft card room where Sherlock and I had arranged to meet (as per his last letter from Avignon to me) after I had come aboard.

He had purchased his ticket and boarded the Majestic two days earlier at the port of Cherbourg France and no doubt had well spent the time from coming aboard to his arrival to meet with me at Southampton reading and studying in great detail about our eventual destination.

As I entered the well appointed but sparingly occupied room I smiled to myself as I saw Sherlock seated (as if still in his study in 221B Baker Street) in a far corner beside a small table oblivious to the others in the room around him holding a book in his right hand quietly reading.

His location was next to a window through which I could still catch the morning view of the varied activities and sights of the docks but I knew it would soon be traded for one of the constantly rising and falling sights of the blues and greens that would be the Atlantic ocean as we steamed our way west.

First noting the varied mix of standing and seated men and women passengers gathered in the card room some engaged in quiet conversation and others in small groups seated around small tables playing various card games…I returned my gaze to Sherlock who was still lost to the world in a small blue cloth bound volume (I would later find out) was titled "A visitors Guide to New York City" written by a Robert H. Wiebe whose other published book was The Search for Order,

I was going to give him a few more minutes to come to the end of the chapter he was involved in before closing the short distance between us and making my presence to him known...when he unexpectedly lowered his book...stood up...regarded me for a moment...warmly smiled and kindly said to me as if we had only parted earlier that morning at Paddington train station "Mary, how good it is to see you again." I returned his smile as I approached him and replied with "Sherlock the south of France has done wonders for you and it is good to see you again too."

Graciously indicating for me to take the seat on the other side of the table where he had been seated, he sat down again placed his guide book down on the table beside him...after seating myself he started by thanking me for my invitation to come to New York City then began to give a brief travelogue of the sights he had seen and places he had visited including the wonderful French cuisine he had experienced during his stay in Avignon.

"Ah Mary...the south of France" he (so out of character) wistfully started...when he was interrupted by a somewhat metallic sounding male voice coming over the ships inside and outside tannoy's (public announcement speakers) announcing. Good morning ladies and gentlemen this is the captain...may I have your attention please...as the ship is about to get underway shortly we would ask at this time that all persons visiting on board please disembark thank you." There was a momentary pause then a more official notice was heard "Attention all deck hands report to your muster stations to make ready to cast off."

Realizing that both Sherlock and I would not be seeing England (much less dry land) for some time we both got up and made our way out from the card room and to the passenger railing of the right or "Star board "side of the promenade deck of the ship.

We joined the other passengers already gathered there in saying their enthusiastic goodbyes down to the loved ones gathered on the pier below who had come to see their friends and family off and all together witness the large and impressive ocean liner depart from its home port.

First far to our left (near to the bow) of those standing along the passenger rail we collectively heard the growing rattling sounds of the two large and substantial chains slowly moving back along the deck indicating that both the Majestic's large and heavy anchors were gradually and noisily being winched up from the bottom of the deep harbour.

Each passing just either side of the ship's bow towards the cat heads (projections near the bow to which the anchors are secured)...then witnessed the canvas topped passenger gang way...our last connection to land being raised and moved away from the side of the ship by two stevedores and at the same time heard the large passenger boarding hatch (just below us) solidly close.

Next we observed the fore…mid ship and aft hawsers or large mooring lines being released from the docks bollards by dock hands then taken up by the crew onboard to be stored on deck,…last feeling the slight vibration beneath our feet indicating the liners steam turbines were starting up causing the four propellers located at the stern of the ship to begin to spin.

With two long and loud blasts of the Majestic's large twin and distinctive deep sounding steam powered horns mounted on the forward funnel to announce our departure we began to slowly move forward.

Under the command of Sir Bertram Hayes (the captain) the massive ship started to slip slowly away (with the tide) from the dock where it had been moored and eventually make its way first south to the English Channel then west out into the vast Atlantic Ocean.

After Sherlock and I witnessed the departure and the last bit of land finally disappear from the oceans horizon we along with others slowly made our way back to the card room.

Once seated again at our table Sherlock finished with his colorful travelogue then displaying his new found knowledge from the book he had been studying noted about our voyage confidently stating "with a brisk wind, favourable ocean currents and a good head of steam we should arrive in about six days to a different world full of new and endless possibilities."

Chapter 2

The unsettled weather conditions (that had over taken us on the Atlantic Ocean shortly after departing from the English Channel that were now occurring day and night had created somewhat hazardous conditions on deck which meant all of our passenger activities were (it was advised for our safety) to be restricted to the indoors.

This gave Sherlock and I a chance to become better acquainted with some of the passengers who were making their return crossing who in turn invited both of us to visit with them while he and I were both on holiday in New York City.

For the first day and evening of the voyage Sherlock and I were able to maintain fairly low and inconspicuous profiles. After all to most of the passengers on board we were only two among many and when we dined with others we were just anonymous and unknown first initials and last names (S. Holmes and M. Watson) each precisely printed in black ink on a small folded white place card.

Each card placed to designate assigned seating for whatever meal and table we would be eating at. It was when Sherlock and I had received a formal invitation on the second night out to dine at Sir Bertram's (the captains) table along with other invited passengers where formal introductions were mandatory that both Sherlock's famous identity as well as mine through association with him (by John) were to be revealed.

The proper introductions (after dessert) had, by the captains request started comfortably with the couple sitting across from me at the large dinner table...who had introduced themselves as Mr. Stan and Mrs. Eileen Moore from Albany New York (where he was employed by the city waterworks department).

When it eventually came around to where it was my turn I calmly rose from my chair...confidently stood for a moment looked around at all seated and so not to attract any unwanted attention chose to simply introduce myself as "I am Mary Watson."

Not waiting for or wanting any possible recognition or acknowledgment of my last name I immediately sat down. There was a pause as I waited for Sherlock in turn to rise and wondered how he might introduce himself to all when one of the dinner guests at the table looked puzzled about my introduction then with some curiosity asked "Mary Watson...I know that name from somewhere are you perhaps the widow of the late Dr. Watson?"

I smiled demurely and quietly answered "yes I was." "Well then" said the inadvertent discoverer of my identity as if he had come to some brilliant deduction "that can only mean by your simple and humble introduction that the gentleman by association sitting to your right must be *the* Mr. Sherlock Holmes."

Then as if one of the dinner guests at the table had already read my thoughts as to what would inevitably follow the last statement I still cringed when I heard the clichéd words in a distinct New York accent say "Coming to America to solve a crime or mystery then Mr. Holmes?"

With a bemused smile I had seen so many times in situations as this before...Sherlock patiently answered "since my identity has now been uncovered and that formal introductions have been dispensed with...my answer to your inquiry is I have come on the voyage merely to keep Mrs. Watson company"... here he paused for a moment then continued serenely while pointing generally in the direction of the large night sea spray soaked dining room windows "and of course to take in the sea air."

As result of that particular dinner for the rest of the journey on board the Majestic, with the exception of solitary time spent in his cabin Sherlock certainly did not lack for company.

Watching him with his newly acquired admiring entourage I wondered how my writer friend Winifred would have dealt with such adoration and fame.

I certainly gave Sherlock credit for the patience he showed with all the new found attention that was directed toward him...but I now knew that he was even more eager for the ship to reach its port of destination more than any of the other passengers on board were.

Chapter 3

During the time we were aboard the Majestic steadily navigating our way west to New York City there was a wealth of activities (including excellent meals such as Creme Chatelaine Boiled Turbot—Shrimp Sauce Lamb Cutlets—Green Peas Roast Duckling—Apple Sauce Baked York Ham—Spinach Cauliflower Roast & Boiled Potatoes Bachelor Pudding Apple Tart Albert Cakes Ice Cream Dessert Coffee, afternoon and evening entertainment and an extensive and well read library all provided by the White Star line to make the time of the voyage feel shorter.

During the days (after luncheon) a good number of dining chairs and a lectern were set up theater style in the spacious carved wood and crystal ceiling lounge for interesting impromptu lectures given by various invited speakers.

One of the first was given by Sir Bertram Hayes was about the history of the steam ship line and the recent lineage of ship we were traveling on. There was C. S. Lewis (*Mere Christianity*) known to his friends and family as "Jack", who is a novelist, poet, academic, literary critic, essayist, and Christian apologist.

As well there were others presenting lectures throughout afternoons on the voyage on what the White Star Line hoped would be stimulating subjects that would be of general interest to the passengers.

For those not interested in the topic being presented that particular afternoon the Majestic provided alternative entertainment in the form of a number of wireless (radio) sets located in the comfortable reading and writing room. With some careful tuning the listener could receive and listen through head phones to any near or far radio broadcasts (including the BBC which had just started broadcasting in 1922) that were within range of the Majestic's wireless receiving antenna.

Our indoor day activities were disrupted only twice during our crossing by mid morning abandon ship drills. This is where all the passengers are required to appropriately dress for the outdoor weather conditions...are issued a flotation jacket by a member of the crew then instructed to assemble at their assigned rain soaked life boat deck stations to be shown how to properly board the rescue vessel.

Then with its precious cargo be safely lowered down to the ocean surface and then safely rowed away from the sinking ship. Since the unfortunate loss of life onboard the RMS Titanic (14 April through to the morning of 15 April 1912) organized life boat drills with the White Star Line (despite the weather) are no longer optional but were now mandatory.

On the first two evenings of the crossing (after dinner) entertainment was provided in the grand theater with two well attended piano concerts one given by the great Sergei Rachmaninoff performing the Hungarian Rhapsody composed by Franz Liszt as well as two other pieces written by the composer Also a piano concert given by Miss Judith Gordon performing Serenade composed by Felix Mendelssohn as well as two other pieces written by the composer.

The following two evenings the passengers were entertained with dramatic readings from present well known authors as Virginia Woolf (*Night and Day*) and F. Scott Fitzgerald (*The Beautiful and the Damned*)...poets E.E. Cummings (*Tulips and Chimneys*) and T.S. Elliot (*Portrait of a Lady*).

The last evening sailing west on a now calm and moon lit Atlantic Ocean we were entertained with a motion picture show. The one that was shown was The Three Musketeers...an American film based on the novel *The Three Musketeers* by Alexandre Dumas, père...starring Douglas Fairbanks as d'Artagnan

Chapter 4

On the last morning of our crossing the weather conditions (although still very grey...overcast and chilly) had somewhat improved enough for the passengers (if they were properly dressed for the outdoors), who wanted to venture out onto the port (left) and starboard (right) promenade decks of the ship to have their last view looking back towards the stern of the ship and the open ocean we were leaving behind.

For most though their first view looking forward from the Majestic's bow of America, more specifically the seemingly vast and growing congregation of impressively tall buildings (known as sky scrapers) that together created the awe inspiring panoramic skyline defining New York City.

Another feature that defined New York City at this time was what was known as "The Noble Experiment," or Prohibition. With the passage of the 18th Amendment to the United States Constitution in 1919, the selling, creating, and moving of alcoholic beverages was made illegal in the U.S. Intended to lessen the "evils" of alcohol, the movement created new ones and new businesses to support it instead.

In New York City during the 1920's, there were some 32,000 of these businesses operating. The source of real alcohol was obtained by smuggling it in from Mexico, The Dominion of Canada, and the West Indies. This trade, known as bootlegging, was becoming quite profitable.

At 5 days, 14 hours and 45 minutes at an average speed of 22.69 knots the White Star Line ship RMS Majestic left the Atlantic Ocean and sailing past Staten Island on our left and Brooklyn on our right entered into New York Harbour.

Again with two long and then with two long and loud blasts of the Majestic's large twin and distinctive deep sounding steam powered horns mounted on the forward funnel this time to announce our arrival while passing Ellis Island then Liberty Island on the left side of the ship our speed was reduced.

With the assistance of two study and powerful tug boats and a pilot (who had come aboard to guide us to our final destination) we left the harbour...entered and made our way slowly up the busy (filled with boat and ferry traffic) Hudson river to finally dock at the New York Passenger Ship Terminal...a terminal for ocean-going passenger ships on Manhattan's west side.

The terminal consists of North River Piers 88, 90, 92 and 94 on the Hudson River between West 46th and West 54th Street...our port of debarkation would be White Star Line pier 94. It should be noted that when the Majestic finally berthed in New York, the ship was so large that forty one feet of its stern projected into the river not flanked by the pier, at the time no pier in New York was long enough to do so.

Even as the huge ocean liner was dropping its two massive and heavy anchors that would both quickly settle to the bottom of the deep river...fore...middle mid and aft hawsers were being secured from the deck above to the dock bollards below and as the green canvas passenger gangway was at last finally and securely in place (allowing passengers to disembark) I could just make out my cousin Alice and her husband Peter.

They were in and among the large waving and cheering multitude of people who had all come to pier 94 to welcome family and friends on board the ship ashore to New York City.

Collecting our carry on luggage Sherlock and I joined an orderly queue comprised of us and the other passengers to leave the liner. As we descended (a little unsteadily at first after being after being on a rolling ship for five days) down the gangway I looked left then right to take in the architectural grandeur and vitality that was New York City.

Then I looked back behind me (at the passengers following Sherlock and me) and was amazed as to how the ship seemed to grow in scale and dimension the closer and nearer as we all got to our final destination.

With our feet firmly planted on the well worn large black paving stones that comprised the dock and waterfront and looking around to get my bearings I could hear my Cousin Alice's distinctive voice through the large and increasingly busy with movement and mixed voices gathering of passengers, friends and family calling "Mary…over here!"

Sighting her and Peter through a gap in the gathering I directed Sherlock in their direction by saying to him "this way." Seeing Alice first…she was as I had remembered her from our last visit. Shoulder length dark auburn hair… emerald green eyes set in a peaches and cream complexioned warm and attractive face. As always attractively dressed and although a bit short in stature she had the assured presence of someone much taller.

Peter her husband (a little taller and than his wife) was still…as Alice once told me just after they had first met "ruggedly attractive with his "quirky smile" and was smartly attired from head to toe as any other successful business man in New York City would be.

After warm family embraces had been exchanged between me…my cousin and her husband formal introductions were in order. Drawing my travelling companion to my side I started "Sherlock…this is my cousin Alice Eastman and her husband Peter."…"Alice and Peter this is my close and personal friend Mr. Sherlock Holmes."

This was one of those times when I was reminded that the friendship Sherlock and I shared was unique as he extended his hand in greeting to both Alice and Peter and stated "it is a pleasure to meet you Mrs. Eastman and you too Mr. Eastman." In turn both Alice and Peter warmly returned the greeting and said "We have heard so much about you from Mary Mr. Holmes ...and welcome to New York City."

With Sherlock's and my luggage now being delivered Peter walked a few paces from where we were standing to the curb...raised his right hand into the busy city traffic passing by us on the street to flag down (as the Americans say) and secure transport that would take all of us from our present location to 156 East Forsyth Street (Forsyth Street was named in 1817 for Lt. Colonel Benjamin Forsyth).

Whereas motor taxi's in London and probably most of England were somewhat box like...uniformly a dark color (usually black) and their distinction from other automobiles on the streets was the for hire sign on their roof that if illuminated meant the motor taxi was available for paying fares.

The vehicle that pulled up in front of us to take us to the Eastman residence was quite different from what Sherlock and I were used to seeing. The first thing I noticed was that the smartly uniformed driver seated on the left side of the vehicle...it was bigger and more rounded in shape than what I was used to riding in ...and the difference that struck me the most was that it was painted yellow.

According to Yellow Cab Co. tradition, the color and name been selected by John Hertz in 1912 as the result of a survey by the University of Chicago which indicated it was the easiest color to spot.

The other unique difference were the words "Yellow Taxicab Co." in two inch high black precisely hand painted letters that stretched the length between the front and rear doors of the automobile.

Just after the company identification came the words in slightly smaller letters "fare 50¢/mile "indicating the rate of hire. With all of us comfortably seated and our luggage stored in the boot or trunk as it was known as of the taxicab...the driver turned his head back in our direction asked with a courteous "where to?" we were on our way across town to Alice and Peter's home.

Chapter 5

Our ride from the White Star pier took us into...among and through constantly in motion busy and noisy automobile, street car and pedestrian traffic (with regular stops and starts for traffic lights) south along (on our right side) what New Yorkers called the "Upper West Side". The Upper West Side is an upscale, primarily a high rise residential area with many of its residents working in more commercial areas in Midtown and Lower Manhattan.

We viewed on our left side (as if to balance the concrete and stone) the expansive length and greenery of Central Park. Central Park (of which Sherlock had learned) was designed by landscape designer and writer Frederick Law Olmsted and the English architect Calvert Vaux in 1858 after winning a design competition.

As well as a moving panorama view of greenery we caught with in the park a quick glimpse of the impressive building that houses The American Museum of Natural History.

When reached the far south end of the park...at the traffic light we made a left hand turn from Central Park West and east onto 59th street to continue the journey.

This well known and travelled street, after crossing the East River would take the four of us from the commercial and business heart of Manhattan to the residential portion of Manhattan and to the community or neighbourhood known as Sunnyside Gardens where Alice's and Peters home was located.

As the taxicab stopped in front of Alice's and Peter's home both Sherlock and I were impressed.   156 East Forsyth Street, Sunnyside Gardens Manhattan New York was by English standards a large detached clap board (painted a light banana cream yellow with accented light blue trim) bay and gable two story home.

Its main striking features were to the left (as you faced the house from the tree lined street) a spacious covered ground level veranda with stairs leading from the walk way to the front door and to the right a first story (parlour) large three paned bay window and second story (master bed room) also a large three paned bay window. Both the veranda and the ground floor bay window areas were lined by low trimmed bushes and surrounded by a green well cared for lawn that extended out from the front of the house to the main sidewalk.

When Sherlock and I, with our luggage being taken care of by Peter entered the house Alice welcomed us to their home then directed us as to which guest room each of us would be staying during our visit. "Mary you will have the second story guest room which is to your left at the top of the stairs." "Mr. Holmes you will be staying in the guest room on the main floor…it is the room opposite to Peters study."

With both of us becoming acquainted with our holiday lodgings, hanging up and putting our respective clothing into dresser draws and dealing with personal toiletry articles Sherlock, I and our hosts met a short time later in the kitchen to be given the grand tour of the Eastman home.

I found that each room in the house was bright and spacious…tastefully decorated and seemed to reflect equally the personal tastes of both Alice and Peter.

After the tour and returning to where we had started Sherlock and I were escorted through the kitchen door that led onto the rear veranda of the house and were shown what Americans call the "back yard".

The "yard" (what we in England would know as a tract of ground next to, surrounding, or surrounded by a building or buildings) was bounded on three sides by a high picket fence painted in the same color as the house and the area it surrounded was carpeted by a green well groomed, level and cared for lawn that was also edged by low trimmed bushes.

To break up the horticultural uniformity and to attract the eye there was a large and mature oak tree growing (which had been there before the house had been built) in an area that occupied a measure of the right rear of the yard.

Standing on the Eastman's veranda enjoying the scenery breathing in and enjoying the fresh evening residential air was a nice change compared to the downtown air that I had been taking into my lungs since departing the Majestic and our taxi ride here. Closing my eyes for a moment I was almost back at 126 Hill House Road when Peter asked "Are we all ready for dinner?"

Realizing that Sherlock's and my last meal (breakfast) had been eaten while still sailing from the Atlantic Ocean into New York Harbour I nodded an enthusiastic yes...so did Alice and Sherlock acknowledged the request by enthusiastically stating "an excellent idea." "Splendid" said Peter smiling "because I made reservations for us to have dinner tonight at the Russian Tea Room which I know you Mary and Mr. Holmes will enjoy. I'll let everyone change and freshen up while I call a taxicab."

The Russian Tea Room founded by members of the Russian Imperial Ballet (a few years earlier), is located at 150 West 57th Street. It exudes the extravagance of the former 19th and early 20th century tsarist Russia. With antique brass samovars, intricately decorated Fabergé eggs and glistening chandeliers, the restaurant possesses a grandeur essence unlike any other.

This was further reflected by the opulent décor our party took in and appreciated as we were being led from the entrance (where Peter had confirmed our reservations) through to where we would take pleasure in eating dinner...and although I did not recognize any of the faces of the other patrons seated at their tables I passed by that evening I felt that I would be among esteemed company while dining.

The Maître' D who had lead us past other lively conversation filled and busy tables stopped in front of a stunningly well set (as of yet unoccupied) one...graciously extended his right hand and announced "Eastman...party of four...your table."

After helping Alice and I to be seated while Sherlock and Peter were seating themselves...he stated "your waiter will be with you shortly to bring you the menu...mesdames et messieurs enjoy your dinner."

The red leather bound menu when presented by our attending waiter was in keeping with the restaurant's luxurious atmosphere, certainly created to lavish our taste buds with Russian and continental cuisine.

The lively and sparkling back and forth conversation taking place at our table that accompanied the appetizer and then sumptuous main course consisted first of life and events in New York city in general of the business life in mid town Manhattan with Peter and the comings and goings of domestic life in Sunnyside Gardens Manhattan with Alice and Peter. With a pause to place cutlery on now empty plates the direction of the conversation then unexpectedly (for me anyway) changed in direction.

"And what of you Mary?" my cousin (to my surprise) turned to me and inquired as the dinner plates and cutlery were now being discreetly removed from our table soon to be replaced by plates and cutlery more suited to a classic Russian dessert.

Not sure just yet as to my place in Sherlock's professional life I thought for a moment then as quickly and as nonchalantly as I could replied knowing that she was waiting for my answer. "I continue to volunteer at the hospital, there is of course is the house to keep up whenever visitors come to London, some evenings I listen to the wireless and other evenings I sit and read John's journals after dinner so in some way he is still with me."

Almost as a fleeting after thought as if to add a bit of substance to my seemingly sparse reply I innocently finished with "and I also occupy myself with a bit of writing."

Thinking that Alice's sudden look of interest at this unexpected disclosure meant that she might want to ask a revealing and specific follow up question that I might not yet have a proper answer for I quickly cut off her anticipated query.

Thinking quickly I answered with "I correspond with a writer friend in Gravesend and I keep a (here I started to use the word journal but quickly and I thought wisely switched to) personal diary. At this point Sherlock who had been quietly following our conversation folded his napkin and placed it on the table in front of him. His response to my hurried answer was to first give me a look of mock disapproval...then shaking his head side to side slightly he said to Alice and Peter in an assured tone "Mrs. Watson sells herself short...while indeed it is true that she writes and corresponds she has now taken up chronicling detective cases...she is in fact the author or chronicler of my most recent case which concerned the affairs of the friend she has just mentioned."

There was a momentary look of surprise that registered in Alice's and Peters face as both took in this astonishing and unexpected news then they turned to Sherlock and to me for confirmation of this bold announcement. Knowing that this surprising statement needed obvious clarification Sherlock continued.

"If you have read any of my published cases you will know that there was one name that was constantly associated with their coming into being...that of John Watson. It was a Study in Scarlet that Watson was so impressed by my handling of the case and so incensed by Scotland Yard's claiming full credit for its solution that he exclaimed: "Your merits should be publicly recognized.

You should publish an account of the case. If you won't, I will for you." I suavely (at the time) responded: "You may do what you like, Doctor." Hence Watson did write the story, presented to the Strand...a monthly magazine published in London as the reminiscences of John H. Watson.

In fact it had not been for Watson's sense of injustice...with the yard constantly taking credit for my detective work...by disregarding my indifference to his request and publishing A Study in Scarlet I would not be where I was today"

Sherlock stopped for a moment as if to pay a silent tribute to my late husband then carried on. "Two years ago I lost a dear friend, comrade and companion, a man who was keen to learn my detective skills and methods, to improve his observational and deductive skills…someone I must say who had an admirable ability to take down notes no matter where he was at.

Looking directly at me he continued "I am a man of habits…and he had become one of them…a comrade…upon whose nerve I could place some reliance…a whetstone for my mind. He stimulated me…If he irritated me by a certain methodical slowness in his mentality, that irritation served only to make my own flame-like intuitions and impressions flash up more vividly and swiftly. Such was his humble role in our alliance."

"With honouring a last request from her husband, Mary has in many ways has taken up the professional role that Watson…I mean John with the void of his passing might have left behind.

When there was no more to be said the arrival and the serving of the Russian dessert Kissel a la Russe provided a convenient silence. Alice after tasting her dessert broke the stillness "Mary I'm so proud of you…John would be honoured" with that Sherlock looked at me warmly to let me know he felt the same way too.

With the eventual clearing of the final dishes and cutlery of the dessert from the table to the waiter discreetly presenting the check for dinner to Peter I now knew my role in Sherlock's professional life.

Chapter 6

It was during the taxicab ride (on our first morning in New York City) from the down town White Star pier to the Eastman's home that Peter had asked both Sherlock and I in passing if we wanted to tour Central park one afternoon during our stay…

Central Park is bordered on the north by West 110th Street, on the south by West 59th Street, on the west by Eighth Avenue. Along the park's borders, these streets are known as Central Park North, Central Park South, and Central Park West respectively. Only Fifth Avenue along the park's eastern border retains its name.

It was designed by Calvert Vaux and Frederick Law Olmsted, and is home to many attractions spread throughout its 843 acres of landscape.

The landmarks nestled in the park are diverse; visitors can find everything from sprawling waters and green meadows to stunning bridges, gardens and even classical architecture.

The park also boasts numerous statues of iconic figures, including Alice and Wonderland and even William Shakespeare; fountains and the oldest public monument in North America: The Obelisk

Central Park is also the home to the famed New York City restaurant Tavern on the Green which is located on the park's grounds at Central Park West and West 67th Street. This was where Alice, Sherlock and I would take lunch later in the day.

After leaving Peter in the taxicab to continue his journey onto his place of business Alice, Sherlock and I entered the park at the Vanderbilt gate located on East 105 Street which is near to the entrance of Central Park's Conservatory Garden.

We turned left departed the world of tall buildings busy pedestrian filled sidewalks and hectic traffic filled roads to begin our leisurely stroll south through manmade and natural wonders…before entering Central Park we took a tour of the conservatory gardens (while admiring the flora and fauna displays) then past the Harlem Meer and down the wide path that closely paralleled 5th Avenue until we arrived at 97th Street.

After the motor traffic had cleared we proceeded to the next part of Central Park that included what was locally known as the reservoir which occupies a good portion of this part of the park.

This large artificially created body of water is a favourite in the winter months for ice skaters to make use of when conditions are right and in the clear summer months for model sail boat enthusiasts to sail their hand built water craft on. After sitting on a nearby park bench to take in an impromptu miniature regatta for a time we then made our way to 85th street.

Crossing the street the three of us were presented with two impressive sights...to our left was the expansive and imposing building the housed the American Museum of Natural History and in front of us and to our right the vast green expanse of manicured green grass creating a series of "meadows" complete with mature trees and semi grass enveloped large rock knolls which collectively and together were known to New Yorkers as the Great Lawn.

As we were walking past Alice told Sherlock and me that this was a favourite area for couples and families to have Saturday and Sunday afternoon picnics during the summer months. Whenever she and Peter had decided to enjoy the Great Lawn they had left the house early in the morning to guarantee them a nicely shaded area to eat the packed lunch and spend the day together

As Alice was telling me this I could envisage small groups and families of picnickers sprinkled all across the area sitting on large blankets opening up and unwrapping all types of outdoor food to partake of and at the same time taking in the company of others nearby while all were enjoying the warm summer day and the gentle breezes wafting around them.

The most important monument in Central Park is Cleopatra's Needle, an authentic Egyptian obelisk, is located east of the Great Lawn. The 65 foot tall granite obelisk was originally erected at Heliopolis and later moved to Alexandria.

In the mid 19th century it was donated to the US as a gift from Egypt. The obelisk stands near the Metropolitan Museum of Art, one of the world's most important museums, with an enormous collection of artwork from all continents, covering a period from prehistory to today.

Crossing 79th Street and still following the same wide path south that paralleled 5th Ave we came to a part of Central park that contained a wooded section of the park called "The Ramble" which is popular among birders. Many species of woodland birds, especially warblers, may be seen in The Ramble in spring and fall. Then we walked past a body of water a little smaller than The Reservoir that was known as "The Lake" where rowboats can be rented on an hourly basis at the Loeb Boathouse.

Then we arrived at our luncheon destination…the Tavern on the Green (a single storied wide U shaped red brick and grey slate roof tiled building with a large already partially occupied outdoor patio.

The three of us would share with others already there a leisurely alfresco lunch and while seated at patio tables and chairs enjoy the weather. While spending time there we could if we chose to casually observe others on the path we had been on making their way past us proceeding north to south or south to north through the park.

The only black cloud that momentarily passed in front sun for me at this time was when a particularly large group of people walked past us from left to right...and for the briefest of moments I was certain I saw among them the face and form of Ashley Laurinda Taggart.

Not sure if I had in fact I seen her or that she had seen me but that both of us had only imagined the incident I made no mention of it to Alice, or especially to Sherlock and put the matter out of my mind.

The mid day menu the restaurant offered included choices such as lobster bisque, smoked salmon, roast chicken or garlic braised spinach. Desserts included crème brulee and cheesecake. Central Park is the home to this famed New York City restaurant which is as located on the park's grounds at Central Park West and West 67th Street.

It's very peculiar that one of New York City's most venerable dining places was founded in the late 1800s to house sheep. The famous Tavern on the Green in Central Park was in fact built to house sheep in 1870 and wasn't converted to serve the city as a restaurant until 1920. Legendary New York Tammany Hall Mayor John F. Hylan opened the restaurant with a brass key. In the last two years Tavern on the Green has become a favourite dining spot for New York City powerbrokers, celebrities and other well-to-do clients.

Our day together a Central Park finished with crossing 65th Street walking together through the final part of the park that contained what was known as The Pond…then leaving through the busy Merchants gate located at Columbus circle where Sherlock with a single attempt managed to "flag down" a passing taxicab in the busy afternoon traffic to take the three of us back to the Eastman residence.

During dinner (broiled chicken, cauliflower, boiled potatoes and Katherine cake) that both Alice and I had prepared Sherlock and I found out as Alice's and Peters way of thanking us for coming to New York city they were taking us out the next evening to The Hippodrome theatre to see a particular favorite of Sherlock's perform.

Chapter 7

The Hippodrome Theatre was built by Frederick Thompson and Elmer Dundy, creators of the Luna Park amusement park at Coney Island, with the backing of Harry S. Black's U.S. Realty, a dominant real estate and construction company of the time, and was acquired by The Shubert Organization in 1909.

It is located on Sixth Avenue between 43rd and 44th Streets in the Theater District of Midtown Manhattan. It is called the world's largest theatre by its builders and has a seating capacity of 5,300, with a 100 x 200 ft. stage.

The theatre has modern theatrical equipment, including a rising glass water tank. Acts which have appeared at the Hippodrome have included numerous circuses, musical revues, vaudeville acts, and silent movies such as *Neptune's Daughter* (1914) and *Better Times* (1922)

As impressive in size and grandeur the red brick and white marbled tiled two storied theatre building was during the day…it was even more so when fully illuminated by what seemed like thousands of small electric lights at night as the four of us got out of the taxicab on 6th avenue to make our way inside the foyer. Stopping momentarily to read the large colourful posted play bill we knew we were in for an evening of amazing entertainment.

GRAND SPECIAL NIGHT
The World Famous Liberator

HOUDINI
The Supreme Ruler of Mystery
MAGICAL REVUE
In which he will prove himself
To be the Greatest Mystifier
that History chronicles
With
The Needle Trick
Good Bye, Winter
Money for Nothing
The Arrival of Summer
The Calico Conjurer
Metamorphosis

8:30 p.m. Tonight
HIPPODROME THEATRE

The four blue crushed velvet theater seats that Peter had reserved for us for the evening's performance were located about mid way along on the first balcony. This would afford us a clear and unobstructed view of the performer on what was an incredibly large and wide stage.

Seeing the building from the outside gave no impression of how vast and spacious the theatres interior was or of the apparent endless sea of empty seats available that would soon be filled with theater goers.

On the taxicab ride over Peter had mentioned to Sherlock and me a number of astonishing facts about the Hippodrome…audience capacity being one…of over 5,000 he had stated…now seated in the theatre and watching the seats all around us in all directions start to fill I began to believe that Mr. Houdini would be playing to a full house

The accommodation in each audience seating area of the theatre was arranged in a gentle curve or arc so in theory there were no bad seats. Without knowing the actual number of people attending from what I could tell where we were located that approximately 1/3 of the audience were seated in the ground floor area (in front of and below us) …1/3 were seated in the large first balcony seating area (where we were) and 1/3 were seated in the sizable second balcony area (up and behind us).

When we had arrived and had been seated the four of us had been able to carry on a conversation…but with the increasing number of people coming in and seating themselves we soon found that with the rising sounds of voices all around us we that had to lean in to each other's direction to be heard.

Just as the sound was starting to become slightly unbearable the house lights were dimmed and there was a descending silence with finally nothing to be heard except for the occasional echo somewhere in the theatre of a cough or of someone trying to clear their throat.

As we were sitting in the darkened theater we with the audience would normally expect performers to enter from a side entrance... "Pomp and Circumstance" to be played... and all of a sudden a big spotlight comes on in the back of the theater and it shines on him... and he comes down through the audience. He was 5'7", but he walked like he was six feet tall in his tails and everything. As the audience saw and recognized him they started clapping   and   clapping.

When he got up on the stage, he turned around and opened up his arms, and they gave him a standing ovation. He didn't do anything yet! It's his charisma. It was so crazy about him....after all on the stage was a small statured...a mere 5'7", man with dark, wavy hair, piercing dark gray eyes dressed in formal evening attire...projecting the noticeable confidence and personality of a seasoned performer.

Harry Houdini's entrance as described by his young niece Marie Hinson

Anticipating a long standing ovation the entertainer quickly introduced himself. "Good evening ladies and gentlemen...and I welcome all of you to the Hippodrome Theatre"... here he paused momentarily for effect...with the applause starting to build again he gave a slight bow of thank you to his many admirers then finished the introduction with "my name is Harry Houdini. Then gesturing to an attractive woman standing next to him he continued "and this is my assistant for tonight's performance...my wife Bess Houdini."

Of the six illusions we saw Mr. Houdini perform that evening two stood out as being spectacular. The first being "The Needle Threading Trick" where his wife came out on stage and first handed him a length of sewing thread which he put in his mouth and appeared to swallow...then she handed him some sewing needles which he also appeared to put in his mouth and swallow.

Pausing for just a minute while the audience dealt with the uncomfortable sensation of such items being painfully forced down their throats...Mr. Houdini reached into his mouth and with confidence pulled out the length of thread from his mouth and to our surprise all of the needles had been threaded on to it.

The last illusion of the evening was certainly the most incredible and unbelievable...while Mr. Houdini was engaged in conversation with some members of the audience two stage hands brought a large and sturdy packing crate out and placed it behind him and Bess Houdini.

"For my final illusion this evening I will perform one I call Metamorphous...where my wife will be bound and placed inside this crate" (here he gestured behind him) there was a gasp of disbelief that went through the audience.

Harry Houdini assured all concerned"please do not be alarmed...she will not come to any harm and will be inside the crate but for only a few short seconds". Continuing he said"the lid of the crate will be closed then secured and I will then take my place on top of it...I will be handed a curtain which I will raise it just above me and when the curtain drops Bess and I will have traded places...she will be safe and unbound standing on top of the crate in my place and I will be bound and inside the still secured crate"

The audience (mostly the women) watched with mixed emotions as Mrs. Houdini was first fitted and bound in a canvas straight jacket then several large chains were wrapped around her each one secured with a sturdy padlock. When it looked like escape for her would be impossible the two stage hands carefully lifted and placed Harry Houdini's wife inside the wooden crate.

As we had been told the lid was closed and secured …then with assistance from the stage hands Harry Houdini climbed up and stood on top of the crate.

He was handed a long and wide blue curtain attached to a horizontal metal pole. Mr. Houdini…being ever the showman taunted the audience by bringing the curtain up to only his waist several times…when we least expected the curtain as had been explained was quickly raised up and over his head.

With that action two things took place…the curtain no longer being held quickly and dramatically fell and landed on to the stage and there to our surprise was Mrs. Houdini (unbound) standing on top of the crate in her husband's place.

When his wife was helped down from the top of the crate and Mr. Houdini was released and unbound the audience in all three sections of the theater rose to their feet and gave both entertainers a five minute standing ovation.

After the performance as we were making our way out of the theater and back to the foyer to collect our coats Peter commented "did you like the show Mary?" I replied "yes very much thank you Alice and Peter."

"And you Mr. Holmes?" With characteristic understatement Sherlock replied "Very entertaining Mr. Eastman thank you. I found Mr. and Mrs. Houdini's illusionary skill and talent very interesting...there no doubt have been times when dealing with certain unsavoury characters that I would like to have employed the talent I saw this evening."

As the four of us now warmly dressed for the late evening weather were standing in front of the closed Hippodrome Theater noting other theater goers also quickly exiting into the cold night we waited and watched the busy and constantly moving tide of street traffic for a passing taxi in the midst to acknowledge us by pulling up next to the curb then take us back to a much warmer 156 East Forsyth Street.

Peter...once inside a warm taxicab with us on its way back to the Eastman's taking Sherlock's earlier comment in the theater for interest asked "Mr. Holmes...would you like to meet Mr. Houdini. He is one of our clients and I am sure that I could arrange for you to meet him while you and Mary are here in New York"

Chapter 8

Spiritism and divination have been around in one form or another since the dawn of mankind's recorded history. During the mid 19th century there was an "explosion" of spiritualistic practice in Europe and the United States.

Although records of spiritualistic practice far predate this time period the Spiritualist movement in the United States brought the beliefs and practices to the fore for the first time in recorded history.

People were swept up in the Spiritualist fad of the time from the most highly educated to common folks, Spiritualism had its hold. Part of the rapid popular ascent of Spiritualism can be attributed to physical effects produced by "mediums" such as spirit knocking, séances, automatic writing, ectoplasmic manifestation, unearthly sounds such as music and voices, levitation and, of course, the photographic 'proof' of ghosts which was purveyed within the successful business of spirit photography.

The Spiritualist movement of the mid 19th and early 20th centuries is much akin to the modern Wiccan and neo-pagan movement of the late 1990s and early 21st century. The early Spiritualist movement was defined by a loosely outlined set of faith-based beliefs and practices that related to communication between the living and the deceased.

Many times this communication was reliant upon paid "professional mediums" who, for a fee, would communicate with the dead. These mediums were the most instrumental part of the rapid growth and success in the Spiritualist movement as they could produce immediate and tangible effects. These mediums could usually create a wide array of effects which were attributed to the spirit presence of the departed.

From humble beginnings the Spiritualist Movement gained a powerful momentum during the 1850s. At the time just before the American Civil War the US Census has indicated that the population of the US was estimated at about 30 million – three million (roughly 10% of the total population) of which claimed to be Spiritualists.

This however, is only a rough estimate as Spiritualism was never formally organized as a religion and it was never intended to be such. In truth the idea of Spiritualism was originally only a diversion to pass the long winter nights as an amusement. As it has been evidenced by history the appeal of Spiritualism as both entertainment and as a physical manifestation of faith took hold and its expansion as a system of belief was imminent

Near Rochester, New York the new found interest of Spiritualism received a pair of its most notable contributors in 1848 – Kate and Margaret Fox. Margaret Fox, eight years of age at the time and her sister Kate, about six-and-a-half claimed to have the ability to communicate with the dead, as was evidenced by strange rapping noises when spirits were purportedly in their presence.

From this point on the Fox sisters were said to have mediumistic abilities and news of such powers spread rapidly. Fuelled by both the faithful spiritualists and endless supply of curiosity seekers the Fox sisters were on their way to being some of the most famous women of their day.

Some four decades later, in 1888, Margaret Fox-Kane came forward to confess that both she and her sister were fraudulent in their practices as spirit mediums. That confession, along with the indictment of spirit photographer William Mumler as a fraud was the beginning of the end of the popular Spiritualist movement.

Although the downfall of the movement began in about 1900 it never completely died out. The movement limped along for a number of years afterward and even experienced a brief revival after World War I. Even with the revival in the 1914 - 1920s eras the movement never really recovered.

Chapter 9

Since 1907 diners in New York City have been enjoying a delicious dining bill of fare at Balthazar. Balthazar…a colourful bistro best known for its sea food is located at 80 Spring Street in the neighbourhood known as Soho.

For those not familiar with Soho is a district located in Lower Manhattan, New York City; it is notable for being the location of many artists' lofts and art galleries. The name "Soho" refers to the area being "SOuth of HOuston (Street)", and is also a reference to the London district of Soho

It was here that Peter had arranged for Sherlock and Harry Houdini to meet for lunch and to get better acquainted with each other. As was his usual habit Sherlock had arrived a little ahead of the arranged time to secure a table where he could take in the bohemian décor and observe the variety of customers in the bistro already enjoying the luncheon fare as well as others as they were entering and leaving the establishment.

After savoring the tantalizing aromas around him of the different types of noon day meals being prepared and served and giving a cursory glance at a different style of lunch menu from what he was used to placing an order from Sherlock looked up and recognized a familiar face and form leave the street…then enter Balthazar.

Unlike as he had been attired at his performance at the Hippodrome this time he was a smartly dressed in tailored light grey business suite...hat and over coat.

Stopping only long enough to remove his hat and coat and hang both up on the stand next to the entrance he shared a few familiar words with a young redheaded female cashier. Harry Houdini then briskly made his way through the noisy lunch time crowded and lively establishment to where Sherlock was already seated waiting for him.

Still steps away Harry Houdini by now had his right hand extended in greeting to shake Sherlock's as he getting up to welcome the performer. "Mr. Holmes...this is indeed a long awaited pleasure!" Harry Houdini said exuberantly..."the pleasure is mine too Mr. Houdini" Sherlock returned with professional admiration.

As they both comfortably seated themselves Harry Houdini picked up the lunch menu knowingly browsed it for a minute looked up and asked Sherlock "Have you decided what you would like to have for lunch Mr. Holmes?"

Sherlock returned with "No this is my first time in the United States Mr. Houdini and the selection of food being offered is certainly far more diverse, interesting and maybe just a bit unfamiliar from what may be available in any public house in Doncaster.

Watching Sherlock wrestle with a vast number of obviously unfamiliar luncheon choices Harry Houdini helpfully inquired "might I suggest something from the South of France?" When the waiter came to the table to take the meal order it was two requests for seared salmon a l'os eille with artichokes, nugget potatoes, carrots and sorre.

While waiting for the meal to arrive Sherlock and Harry Houdini shared some aspects of their professional lives. Sherlock with the more interesting cases and criminals he had encountered that John had chronicled…and Harry Houdini with some of his more spectacular illusions and the stages of where they had been performed.

Chapter 10

When the lunch meal was served the two men ate together in respectful silence…but through many years of sitting across from and observing potential clients in his study in London Sherlock knew there were a number of questions forming in his luncheon companions mind.

Putting his fork down on his luncheon plate for a moment Harry Houdini asked "Mr. Holmes…with past respect to Doctor Watson and present respect to Mrs. Watson although both are excellent chroniclers of your cases as far as I can recollect neither has made any mention of the real dangers you must sometimes face when dealing with particularly malevolent individuals."

Sherlock also put his fork down…thought back into the past and answered "There was one time Mr. Houdini in a case that Dr. Watson had titled *The Final Problem*".… "As I remember his narrative...

I arrived at his (Doctor Watsons) home one evening in a somewhat agitated state and with grazed and bleeding knuckles. I had apparently escaped three murder attempts that day after a visit from Professor Moriarty.

I should stop here for a moment Mr. Houdini and explain this person to you. Professor James Moriarty is a character in the two of the chronicles written by Doctor Watson. He is a criminal mastermind who I would describe as the Napoleon of crime."

"To continue…Moriarty warned me to withdraw from my pursuit of justice against him to avoid any regrettable outcome. First, just as I was turning a street corner, a cab suddenly rushed towards me and I just managed to leap out of the way in time. Second, while I was walking along the street, a brick fell from the roof of a house, just missing me.

I then called the police to search the whole area but could not prove that it was anything other than an accident. Finally, on my way to Watson's house, I was attacked by a thug armed with a cosh. I managed to overcome my assailant and handed him to the police but admitted that there was virtually no hope of proving that the man was in the employ of the criminal mastermind."

"I had been tracking him and his agents for months and was on the brink of snaring them all and delivering them to the dock. Moriarty I should also tell you is the criminal genius behind a highly organized and extremely secret criminal force and I will consider it the crowning achievement of my career if only I can defeat him. Moriarty is out to thwart my plans and is well capable of doing so, for he is, as I admit, the intellectual equal."

"I had asked Watson to come to the continent with him, giving him unusual instructions designed to hide his tracks to Victoria station. I was not quite sure where they will go; this seems rather odd to Watson. I, certain that I had been followed to his friend's house, and then made off by climbing over the back wall in the garden. The next day Watson follows my instructions to the letter and finds himself waiting in the reserved first class coach for his friend, but only an elderly Italian priest is there. The cleric soon makes it apparent that it was me in disguise."

"As the train pulled out of Victoria, I spotted Moriarty on the platform, apparently trying to get someone to stop the train. I was forced to take action as Moriarty had obviously tracked Watson, despite extraordinary precautions. Watson and I alighted at Canterbury, making a change to our planned route.

As we are waiting for another train to Newhaven a special one-coach train roars through Canterbury, as I suspected it would. It contains Moriarty, who has hired the train in an effort to overtake me. Watson and I were forced to hide behind luggage."

"Having made our way to Strasbourg via Brussels, the following Monday I received a message that most of Moriarty's gang had been arrested in England and recommended Watson return there now, as I would likely prove to be a very dangerous companion. Watson, however, decided to stay with me.

Moriarty himself has slipped out of the grasp of the English police and is obviously with them on the continent."

"Our eventual journey took us to Switzerland where we stayed at Meiringen. From there we fatefully decide to take a walk which would include a visit to Reichenbach Falls, a local natural wonder. Once there, a boy appears and hands Watson a note, saying that there is a sick Englishwoman back at the hotel who wants an English doctor. I realized at once it is a hoax although I did not say so. Watson went to see about the patient, leaving me alone."

"When he reaches the *Englischer Hof*, the innkeeper has no knowledge of any sick Englishwoman. Realizing at last that he has been deceived, Watson rushes back to Reichenbach Falls but finds no one there, although he does see two sets of footprints going out onto the muddy dead end path with none returning.

There is also a note from me, explaining that I knew the report Watson was given to be a hoax and that I was about to fight Moriarty, who has graciously given me enough time to pen the last letter. Watson sees that towards the end of the path there are signs that a violent struggle has taken place and there are no returning footprints. It is all too clear Moriaty and I had both fallen to our deaths down the gorge while locked in mortal combat. Heartbroken, Dr. Watson returned to England."

At this point in Sherlock's narrative Harry Houdini commented "Well that would have certainly been the end of your career how did you survive?" "To paraphrase the American writer Mark Twain Mr. Houdini, the rumours of my death were greatly exaggerated." Here Sherlock let a knowing smile play briefly across his face... "as Watson sets out in his account The Adventure of the Empty House only the few members of Moriarty's gang and my older brother Mycroft knew that I was still alive, having won the struggle at Reichenbach Falls that had sent Moriarty to his death – though nearly meeting my own at the hands of Moriarty's henchmen.

As the now empty lunch plates and cutlery were being removed and a pot of tea (at Sherlock's request) along with cream, sugar and two cups and saucers were being placed between the two men Sherlock returned Mr. Houdini's question. "Well Mr. Holmes my situation is not as harrowing or as threatening as yours but with what I have been pursuing I have made a few enemies.

Before I relate my tale to you let me begin with what is known as the principles of spiritualism. There is a belief in spirit communication...a belief that the soul continues to exist after the death of the physical body...Personal responsibility for life circumstances...Even after death it is possible for the soul to learn and improve...a belief in a God, often referred to spiritualists as Infinite Intelligence...and the natural world considered as an expression of said intelligence

Spiritualists...Mr. Holmes believe that they can communicate with the spirits of discarnate humans...from the desperately wanting to believe to the blindly trusting the answers revealed from their dearly departed (to them) are true and authentic...however in my estimation any messages obtained in any way and in any form by spiritualists amount to no more than stage trickery...or at best side show magic.

These sad, lost and lonely people believe that spirit mediums are humans gifted to do this, often through séances. Anyone may become a medium through study and practice. They believe that spirits are capable of growth and perfection, progressing through higher spheres or planes.

The afterlife is not a static place, but one in which spirits evolve. The two beliefs—that contact with spirits is possible, and that spirits may lie on a higher plane—lead to a third belief, that spirits can provide knowledge about moral and ethical issues, as well as about God and the afterlife. Thus many members speak of *spirit guides*—specific spirits, often contacted, relied upon for worldly and spiritual guidance.

In the 1920s Harry Houdini had turned his energies toward debunking self-proclaimed psychics and mediums, a pursuit that would inspire and be followed by later-day conjurers. Houdini's training in magic allowed him to expose frauds that had successfully fooled many scientists and academics.

He is a member of a Scientific American committee that offered a cash prize to any medium who could successfully demonstrate supernatural abilities. None were able to do so, and the prize was never collected. The first to be tested was medium George Valentine of Wilkes Barre, Pennsylvania.

As his fame as a "ghost buster" grew, Houdini took to attending séances in disguise, accompanied by a reporter and police officer. Possibly the most famous medium whom he debunked was Mina Crandon, also known as "Margery".

These activities had cost Harry Houdini the friendship of a famous English detective novel author who is a firm believer in Spiritualism and during his later years refused to believe any of Houdini's exposés.

The famous author came to think that Houdini was a powerful spiritualist medium, and had performed many of his stunts by means of paranormal abilities and was using these abilities to block those of other mediums that he was "debunking" This disagreement led to the two men becoming public antagonists and led the author and others in the movement to view Houdini as a dangerous enemy.

As to the why of all of this you may ask Mr. Holmes? From my early career as a mystical entertainer I have been interested in Spiritualism as belonging to the category of mysticism, and as a side line to my own phase of mystery shows I have associated myself with mediums, joining the rank and file and held séances as an independent medium to fathom the truth of it all.

At the time I appreciated the fact that I surprised my clients, but while aware of the fact that I was *deceiving* them

I did not see or understand the seriousness of trifling with such sacred sentimentality and the baneful result which inevitably followed. To me it was a lark. I was a mystifier and as such my ambition was being gratified and my love for a mild sensation satisfied.

After delving deep I realized the seriousness of it all. As I advanced to riper years of experience I was brought to a realization of the seriousness of trifling with the hallowed reverence which the average human being bestows on the departed, and when I personally became afflicted with similar grief I was chagrined that I should ever have been guilty of such frivolity and for the first time realized that it bordered on crime.

As a consequence my own mental attitude became considerably more plastic. I too would have parted gladly with a large share of my earthly possessions for the solace of one word from my loved departed-just one word that I was sure had been genuinely bestowed by them-and so I was brought to a full consciousness of the sacredness of the thought, and became deeply interested to discover if there was a possible reality to the return, by Spirit, of one who had passed over the border and ever since have devoted to this effort my heart and soul and what brain power I possess.

In this frame of mind I began a new line of psychical research in all seriousness and from that time to the present I have never entered a séance room except with an open mind devoutly anxious to learn if intercommunication is within the range of possibilities and with a willingness to accept any demonstration which proves a revelation of truth.

It is this question as to the truth or falsity of intercommunication between the dead and the living, more than anything else, that has claimed my attention and to which I have devoted years of research and conscientious study.

A famous advocate and follower says in one of his lectures: "When one has a knock at the door, one does not pause, but goes further to see what causes it and investigates, and sooner or later one discovers that a message is being delivered.

So I have gone to investigate the knocks, but as a result of my efforts I must confess that I am farther than ever from belief in the genuineness of Spirit manifestations and after twenty-five years of ardent research and endeavour I declare that nothing has been revealed to convince me that intercommunication has been established between the Spirits of the departed and those still in the flesh.

I have made compacts with fourteen different persons that whichever of us died first would communicate with the other if it were possible, but I have never received a word. The first of these compacts was made more than twenty-five years ago and I am certain that if anyone of the persons could have reached me he would have done so.

When the last of the meal had ended Harry Houdini rose from the table and said apologetically "I don't mean to rush off Mr. Holmes but I have to return to the theatre to set up for this evening performance. However I would like to continue our conversation and I know that Bess, my wife and I would like to have the pleasure of yours and Mrs. Watson's company for dinner at our home sometime soon.

"I'll have her telephone Mrs. Watson at the Eastman's to make the arrangements. Sherlock then also rose from the table...while firmly shaking Harry Houdini's hand stated "It has been a pleasure meeting you Mr. Houdini and I look forward to talking with you again...and also to meeting Mrs. Houdini."

Chapter 11

While Sherlock and Harry Houdini were sharing a lunch together at the local Soho bistro Alice and I were enjoying the same in her kitchen at 156 East Forsyth Street. During the course of the light meal Alice had brought me up to date with life with her and Peter and I in turn shared some of my recent adventures in Gravesend with my friend Winifred and in particular the troubling experiences in a London market I had with the young lady named Ashley Laurinda Taggart.

Again with that previous afternoon in Central Park momentarily crossing my mind again and not too sure if I had only imagined the passing encounter with Miss Taggart and myself I again decided not to bring up the subject.

But fate had already played a hand in recent events and before too long the young lady without my knowledge had escaped justice in London and found her way to New York City to explore a new and far more lucrative avenue of crime. What I thought of at the time as only my imagination playing tricks on me would turn out to be all too real.

I must say at this point in my visit to New York city that when Sherlock and I had sailed from Southampton I safely assumed that Miss Taggart was securely in custody and had bccn subject to the due process of criminal law…subsequently found guilty of the offences of pick pocketing abduction and kidnapping and was now serving an appropriate gaol sentence for her crimes.

However through a combination of skillfully played feigned innocence…beguiling charm and criminal talents she had acquired from her life of crime the young lady had escaped her incarceration. Once free she hurriedly made her way by train from London to Liverpool boarded what known as tramp steamer registered as the SS Flamsteed owned by The Liverpool, Brazil and River Plate Steam Navigation Co. Ltd that would by its circuitous route eventually bring her to America.

I should stop here for a moment and explain to the reader the nature of Miss Taggart's transport. A ship engaged in the tramp trade is one which does not have a fixed schedule or published ports of call. As opposed to freight liners, tramp ships trade on the spot market with no fixed schedule, itinerary or ports-of-call(s).

It is interesting to note that the crews of such ships conveniently make few if any inquiries about the nature or reason of any person who is seeking passage on board because all passengers pay in cash.

A steamship engaged in the tramp trade is sometimes called a tramp steamer; the similar terms tramp freighter and tramper are also in use. The term is derived from the British meaning of "tramp" as itinerant beggar or vagrant; in this context it is first documented in the 1880s, along with "ocean tramp" (at the time many sailing vessels engaged in.)

Chapter 12

The comings and goings of Ashley Laurinda Taggart after arriving in New York City were for a time a mystery. But within a short period she was to become one of the most extraordinary fake mediums and mystery swindlers the United States would ever know. Some would come to class her among the ten most prominent and dangerous female criminals of her time, and her repertoire was claimed to run the full gamut from petty confidence games to elaborately contrived schemes aimed at the magnates of Wall Street.

According to reports she did not hesitate to victimize the innocent and the mentally unsound and left behind her a trail of sorrow, depleted pocket-books, and impaired morals that have seldom been equalled. The marvellous tact with which she devoted her great powers to the purposes of self aggrandizement and profit was without parallel, and for cunning knavery, others in her field, by comparison, seem to have been amateurs.

It is alleged that her crimes ranged from the smallest to the largest with morals as low as one can imagine in a human being while, worst of all, she flaunted this viciousness openly, making no effort whatever to cloak her wickedness and deceit.

Her name would come to stand out with Harry Houdini as being among the half score or more in the front ranks of the history of Spiritualism and with Daniel Dunglas Home (*Daniel Dunglas Home 1833 – 1886 was the forerunner of the mediums whose forte was fleecing by presuming upon the credulity of the subject.*) share the palm for the successful manipulation of big schemes.

It would not come to be unusual for her to make deals that ran into the hundreds of thousands of dollars and though Daniel Dunglas Home was early in the mediumistic field, I believe that to this day they both would have had no peer in this respect. Possibly all other mediums combined could not have aggregated the amount of money as would obtained by these two.

Chapter 13

Suppose a medium comes to your city. He or she (in this case) acquires suitable accommodations then advertises locally that they are available for private séances. Like the average person you are curious (or desperate) and wish to be told things about yourself which you honestly believe no one in the world knows about not even your most intimate friend.

Perhaps you would like to learn some facts about a business deal, or know what is to be the outcome of a love affair, or it may be that you seek the comfort and solace that one is hungry for after the death of a near one. You go to this medium and are astounded by the things which are told you about yourself

It is seldom that one of these mediums will see a person the day he (or she) calls but will postpone the séance from a day or two to a week or more. As the person leaves the building he (or she) is followed by one of the medium's confederates who gather enough information about him to make the medium's powers convincing when the séance is held.

Until Mr. Houdini became involved in the matter of Miss Taggart's new found profession I knew little about mediums. Among the things I would later find out that the stock-in-trade of these frauds is the amount of knowledge they can obtain.

It is invaluable to them and they will stop at nothing to gain it. Mediums' campaigns are planned a long time ahead. They make trips on steamers gathering, tabulating and indexing for future reference the information to be overheard in the intimate stories and morsels of scandals exchanged in the smoking rooms, card rooms, and ladies' salons.

They will take into account the death notices in the newspapers; catalogue the births and follow up the engagement and marriage notices; employ those young people looking for work to attend social affairs and mix intimately with the guests, particularly the women. It was under these unlikely circumstances that the paths of Harry Houdini, his wife Bess, their niece Marie Hinson (asking about a dearly departed one) and Ashley Laurinda Taggart's would fatefully cross.

...

The local residents, vendors and shop keepers who called Wooster Street in Greenwich Village home took little notice as the large precise hand lettered sign advertising " apartment 4 d for rent" was being removed (again) from the street front window of 141...being a four story non descript working class tenement building. But were very curious as to the character of the soon to be new tenet when a day later a large dark green moving van was witnessed pulling up and stopping at the entrance to unload the newest tenets worldly possessions.

Getting out of the cab of the van from the left side were first one then another (for the most part nondescript) movers wearing coveralls, caps and work boots who both silently made their way to the back of the large van to open up its doors then start conveying (as they had done many times before) the small and medium sized every day household items from inside the van to the front entrance of the tenement building.

Alighting from the right (curb) side of the van for the entire street to see and guess about was the appearance of a modestly dressed young lady of a petite build, short stature with long raven black hair and what appeared (when glanced at) to be dark, soul less and bottomless eyes.

Nobody would have guessed that only recently young she had been living with her family above a butcher shop on Welbury Street in Hackney, a working class district, in North London and to escape impending justice along with other criminal reasons had quickly decided leave and relocate to New York City.

Chapter 14

Early one evening in a brownstone located at 278 W 113 Street in Harlem there were four people...the host...his wife and two famous invited dinner guests about to sit down to what would be a very cordial dinner but by the time the invited guests were saying their final "good nights" to their hosts old and forgotten problems for some would present themselves again in new and troubling forms.

After being escorted from the parlour into a warm, cozy and certainly inviting dining room Harry Houdini directed Sherlock and I to our set places at their large oak dining table...while he was attending to his duties as host Bess Houdini was making trips from the large kitchen to bring with her (on the return trips) bowls and serving plates each of what was starting to look like and have the tantalizing smells of a wonderful home cooked meal.

First was a clear soup...then roast rolled fore quarter of lamb...roasted potatoes with gravy...and peas with mint. With the last serving dish placed in the middle of the dining table Bess Houdini took her seat facing her husband who was at the head of the table with Sherlock on his right and me on his left.

She looked a bit uncertain as she started to customarily ask "Mr. Holmes would you like to"... seeing her husband's head shake slightly she asked a little more confidently "Mrs. Watson would you care to say grace?" Not sure as to the denominations that were represented at the table I settled for a neutral "May we give thanks for what we are about to receive." With a collective "amen" the meal began.

The interesting, stimulating and thought provoking dinner conversation that accompanied the meal was centered around the various interests, careers and experiences that was unique to each of us seated at the table that evening.... with all of us in turn sharing some part of ourselves then follow-up comments and occasionally a qualifying question asked from the guests at the table.

The lively dialogue was interspersed from time to time by our host and hostess asking Sherlock and me how we liked the food and if we wanted another serving of the roast or of the main or side dishes that were served with it. After we had each finished our story...exhausted our subjects of conversation the final words heard in the in the Houdini dining room soon faded away to a comfortable silence as the main course was quietly being finished.

Seeing the last fork and knife being placed on now empty (as a show of appreciation) dinner plates by her satisfied guests Bess Houdini rose from her seat...and while collecting the dinner plates...utensils as well as serving bowls and plates from around the table which all would make their way to the kitchen she brightly asked to break the silence "Are we all ready for coffee and dessert?"

As she passed by her seated husband for the last time she gently placed her left hand on his right shoulder and I noticed that an expression had passed between them that some would have taken as a questioning look. I immediately recognised it as the one I used to give John when I wanted to know if it was correct to bring up a question (in polite company) that might be taken as an imposition. Harry Houdini's assured and silent reply to his wife told her "yes."

With that Bess Houdini proceeded to the kitchen and returned with dessert. All of us at the table enjoyed the approaching aroma of the still warm golden baked pastry and cinnamon spiced apple pie...accompanied with thick slices of bright orange cheddar cheese that was served on a decorative wooden serving tray. Then she returned once more this time with a silver tray on it was a white porcelain coffee pot...with four matching cups saucers...spoons cream and sugar. After placing dessert and coffee on the table she returned to her seat.

For moment like an actress or an actor on stage who has forgotten their next line in the play Bess Houdini sat silent oblivious to the dessert and the coffee she had just brought to the table. Then lovingly given a silent cue from her husband she (as in remembering the next line) said "Mr. Holmes I don't mean to impose, and I am not usually in the habit of asking advice from invited dinner guests but because of your well published reputation I have a pressing question to ask. It concerns our niece Marie and her association with a young lady known as Ashley Laurinda Taggart and I…I mean we both wondered if you knew anything about her and her business."

Sherlock and I looked at each other from across the table and we both flashed back to the events that had taken place in Gravesend then London…in particular to Winfred and "The Survivor's List". There was a momentary pause…Sherlock (not knowing of all my encounters with her) confidently smiled at me looked towards Bess Houdini then answered "I believe that Mrs. Watson may be able to provide some details about her."

I admit that when all eyes at the dinner table were focused on me in anticipation of what I might know and reveal I felt conflicted with what I taken be an absolute certainty when I had left Southampton and with the new somewhat disturbing information I had just heard…at the same time I felt a coldness come over me with the realization that is was not just my imagination but in fact it had been Miss Taggart I had seen walking on the path that day at Central Park.

The question that flashed through my mind as I was collecting my thoughts while preparing to relate what little I knew…had Miss Taggart seen me and if she had did she recognize who I was ?

Chapter 15

Marie was puzzled when Sarah…her closest friend at Beekman Paper and Card Company the business where they both were employed…looked distressed while passing a folded note to her the contents of which read it had over heard that a man who looked somewhat like Marie's fiancé had been struck by a street car while he was rushing to cross a busy Fifth Avenue while returning to his place of work.

Suddenly feeling as if her world had dropped away she knew where she should be and it wasn't standing here holding a distressing note. But despite Marie's pleadings the floor manager made it clear that Marie could not leave to go to the hospital to find out what might have happened until the end of her shift.

Rereading the note to know which hospital to go to while suffering an agonizingly long and seemingly slow almost empty of passengers street car ride she finally arrived at the admitting ward of the New York Methodist Hospital to ask to see her fiancé…only to be coldly informed by an attending nurse that because she was not immediate family she wasn't allowed to.

Marie in desperation pleaded with the nurse for any information...seeing the agony in Marie's eyes the nurse reluctantly told her that a street fatality had been brought in earlier in the day but had died a short time later.

With scant information to go forward with Marie blindly made her way to...then sat down in the large...mostly unoccupied cold and impersonal reception area not sure as to what her next steps would be or where to turn.

It was only when nightfall had finally arrived and the ceiling lights were switched on that a nurse noticing her had stopped in front of Marie long enough to say "I'm sorry but you can't stay here...you will have to go" that Marie got up...buttoned her coat then leaving the hospital with mixed emotions went out into the indifferent busy evening street to make her way to the familiar train station and home.

Home was located in a very quiet, safe and calm neighbourhood. She had rented an apartment there because it was very convenient and close to the train station which made it an easy to commute into work each day. Number 1a - 67th Ave., Queens (between Yellowstone Blvd. and 108 St.) was also located very close to a variety of stores and super markets.

It should be explained to anyone who has not been not been to the United States that a supermarket is a large form of the traditional grocery store, it is a self-service shop offering a wide variety of food and household products, organized into aisles. It is larger in size and has a wider selection than a typical traditional grocery store.

Her small but comfortable accommodation consisted of a single room that had two curtained windows which was very convenient to air out the room when most wanted. It included a built-in closet as well as a bed and night table. There was one common bathroom and small kitchen which she shared with another tenet. Her electricity and water use were also included in the rent.

Because the land lord had stated in the advertisement that "A woman is preferable to be a candidate for this room" with her employment references as well as references from her famous uncle and aunt Marie's occupancy had been accepted right away.

Chapter 16

Trying…as John had always advised me…never to come to any conclusions about a suspect until you had all the relevant facts at hand. He had said "it is a capital mistake to theorize before you have all the evidence. It biases the judgment."

I related my experiences (as I knew them) concerning Miss Taggart. The first had taken place at the Gravesend fete…then in front of Munn's (a stationary store) located on the high street in Gravesend…then at the East Street Market in London and lastly more as a reference as I was bidding Sherlock goodbye at Paddington train station.

I had shared a newspaper heading with him and I remember saying "Sherlock I happened to glance at a newspaper this morning and saw that Miss Taggart had been arrested. Apparently she made the mistake of pick pocketing an off duty police constable and now she is awaiting trial."

To finish I said as much to myself as to the people seated at the table his reply "I have a feeling with such persons as her, justice may be cheated for a time but eventually served." In a prophetic way Sherlock had been half right concerning Miss Taggarts presence in New York City and of her new life in crime only I did not know if or when justice would ever be served.

I looked across at Sherlock to see if what I had just related might have sparked a flame in his mind. He pressed his steepled fingers to his lips for a moment and looked as if he was in deep thought…then lowering his hands he observed "it would seem that all of us gathered here tonight in some way have an interest concerning these two curiously connected matters.

Sherlock paused again for a moment then continued…"Mr. Houdini…Mrs. Houdini do either of you have any knowledge of what may have happened recently in your niece's life that may have caused her to seek out Miss Taggarts spiritual help?"

Chapter 17

Trevyn James Craddock (some had noted that he had been a handsome looking gentleman) was born, raised and educated in St. David's Wales. When Great Britain had declared war on Germany in 1914 he enlisted and served as a private in the British I Corps under the command of Field Marshal Douglas Haig.

Demobilized in 1918 he left his home in economically weakened Wales for London to find gainful employment. Trevyn travelled about 200 miles south east to work at a series of menial jobs in a variety of trades until contacted in the spring of 1921 by friends of the family living in the United States who offered him a full time paid position.

Giving notice to his latest employer he packed his few belongings and relocated to New York City that summer to take up the post of junior clerk in the accounting firm Arthur Andersen & Co.

He had met Marie at The Hippodrome Theater during a Saturday afternoon matinee he attended of her famous uncle's performance.

This of course was not the first time she had been there when she was younger she would go with her mother. Marie one time had reminisced to Trevyn about this "I'd go to the theater, and we always sat in the same place... on the first floor. There was a big orchestra...

It would be a three-hour show, and there wouldn't be anyone else on the program just him. The first part of the show, he would do magic. Then he would go off... and somebody would come out or sing or something. When I was there, then he'd come out on stage in a smoking jacket... and say "I have a little niece that I want you to meet. She's in the audience." Meanwhile, my mother's fixing me up... And he'd say, "Is Marie here?"

The two young people had found themselves seated together by accident and during the performance they had both felt the spark of a mutual attraction towards each other then had struck up a friendly conversation together during the intermission.

After the performance Trevyn had nervously invited Marie to share a late afternoon lunch with him at the Midtown Restaurant located on 155 East 55th Street... she accepted and this was where the couple first became better acquainted. They had only been keeping company for a short time when Marie received the troubling note from her friend Sarah concerning Trevyn.

Just after Trevyn James Craddock had finished his lunch he was returning back to work. He had planned that after leaving for the day he was going to spend time with Marie in the evening.

At just the right moment when they arrived at their favorite part of Central Park he was going to ask her to be his bride. This moment never came to be because by crossing the street without looking first and not seeing the oncoming street car until it was too late this tragically ended one life and totally devastated another.

In the back pages of The Daily News (a locally published New York tabloid news paper) buried in among the many tightly spaced advertisements (some with accompanying half tone pictures) for such everyday items as bicycles...comfortable shoes...cough syrup...famous hams and bacon...instantaneous chocolate...photographic apparatus...reservoir pens and stove polish was one that because of what it claimed caught a distraught young woman's attention it read...

"Are you searching for peace of mind...answers to unresolved questions...does happiness and joy elude you? As an experienced spiritual medium I have the answers you seek and I can help to find whatever you are seeking...the past, present and future revealed...telephone Bry 2424 for an appointment. "

...

The next day during lunch break…a telephone call was placed from the Beekman Paper and Card Company managers office (with his permission)…and was shortly answered in Greenwich Village by a competent female voice...that expressed over the telephone what sounded like genuine sympathy and understanding for the callers concerns.

When the conversation ended a fee for the service was suggested and mutually agreed upon…finally an appointment had been set that was to be kept one week later.

Chapter 18

Well before Marie kept her appointment the medium was already well prepared for the visit. Besides employing her usual methods to gather relevant information to impress her new client about her spiritualist skills she had sent one of her accomplices to Marie's place of employment to find out what she could about the young lady and her recent loss.

Here the associate had struck gold…initially in spite of finding out very little about Marie's personal life Sarah, Marie's friend without knowing who she was confiding in showed the accomplice a ribbon bound collection of notes that had passed between Marie and Trevyn

The final important material was gathered by the medium that employed a quiet couple for the express purpose of attending funerals, in this case a particular funeral. The plan was for them to mix with the mourners, and while under the false pretence of offering condolences to those in attendance at the funeral glean any information which would eventually return to 141 Wooster St. Apt. 4 d in Greenwich Village

---

Having been instructed before arriving Marie was told to enter the building where Ashley lived...climb the stairs and then announce her presence.

Hearing a soft knock on the door frame Ashley looked from her chair in the direction of the sound and seeing Marie with some uncertainty standing and waiting at the threshold responded with "Miss Hinson please come in and have a seat" Ashley watched as her newest prize make her way from the open door and into the apartment. "Thank you Miss Taggart" Marie returned a little nervously...still wondering what she might have talked herself into.

Crossing the threshold Ashley guided her visitor to sit at a chair on the right side of a small clothed covered round table...Ashley got up to close the parlour door then returned and sat down in her chair opposite to the chair Marie now occupied ...fixed a gaze on her and appeared to be reading Marie's very thoughts.

Marie…to break the uncomfortable silent scrutiny focused her attention on the room she now found herself in trying to get some fix on whom and what this medium was all about.

The first thing she noticed that despite the fact that as she had made her way to the appointment it had been a warm and sunny day yet all the widows in the room were shrouded with thick almost ceiling to floor red brocade curtains their apparent sole duty to bar all natural daylight passing from the outside to the interior.

The two solitary sources of light in the room was a small multi faceted crystal chandelier suspended from a fixture in the center of the apartment ceiling and a medium sized brass floor lamp (along with the table and chairs being the only furniture in the room) standing silent guard in an opposite corner of the parlour.

She noticed with some curiosity that its large cream hued circular shaped lamp shade appeared to be oriental in nature because it had been hand decorated with bright water color paints as if to perhaps illustrate some exotic story

Closely inspecting her surroundings Marie noticed that the walls (oddly bereft of any pictures) and the ceiling appeared to her to be of the same colour and texture as the curtains…giving Marie the feeling of being surrounded and at the same time almost insulated from the outside world.

She noted that other than the exotic lamp shade the only other colour in the room came from the Persian rug she had first trod on when being invited to enter and was now sitting on in a chair.

Having surveyed the room and not finding any clues about the person sitting in front of her in an effort to break the mediums intense gaze Marie asked a bit uncertainly "So is the room where you contact the departed?"

Ashley smiled a satisfied smile and broke her gaze…already knowing what she needed to know. Graciously she replied "Any room will do Miss Hinson as long as I have this" here she reached down and dramatically started to remove a white silk handkerchief from an object on the table sitting between them that Marie had not taken immediate inventory of…as the silk handkerchief was tantalizingly pulled up and away by mediums delicate hand it revealed a large crystal ball that was nestled in a dedicate and ornate pewter cradle.

Ashley gently placed both of her hands…one on either side of the orb…looked intently at Marie then shifting her gaze to the interior of the clear object she was now lightly grasping then asked in a low voice "who is it that you seek to contact?"

Not having any knowledge of what had taken place that afternoon between the two…some time later I asked Mr. Houdini about how and why a medium might employ a crystal ball.

"The appearance of successful scrying (reading)" he started "depends on the created mood and atmosphere. Above all else, the reader should do not appear to force themselves into a reading session when they don't feel like it. This of course makes little or no difference to the one seeking answers."

"Most readers find crystal ball gazing is easiest when done in a quiet, dimly lit room. Many like to have candles burning. For some the reflections of the flames help to summon images - others find them a distraction.

Burning incense is common and some readers like to have soothing music gently playing from a gramophone in the background. The important thing to remember is to create a believable atmosphere. If someone walked in unexpectedly...not that they would be allowed to, they should instantly be aware that something significant is taking place."

The method that follows he told me is simply what works for most and is taken as a starting point. "Place the crystal on a table in front of you. Many crystal balls you can buy come with their own stand. If you don't have a stand you might like to use a small cushion or a silk handkerchief purchased and reserved specially for this purpose."

"Sit down and relax. Lay your hands gently on the ball for a minute or two in order to energise it and strengthen your psychic rapport. Whilst holding the crystal ball, think about the purpose of this scrying (reading) session. If appropriate try to visualise the subject of your question. Some readers like to ask the question out loud, others find the process works best if they internalise it."

"Now, remove your hands from the crystal. Look into the crystal, stare deeply. Allow your eyes to relax and become slightly unfocussed. After a little while you should see a mist or smoke forming in the crystal. Let this mist grow and fill the ball, then visualise it gradually clearing to reveal images within the crystal."

"The images you appear to see might not be what you expected. That's OK, don't fight them. Your subconscious mind knows what information you need. Just let the images flow, changing and taking you wherever they choose to go. Don't try to rationalise now, time for that later."

"Once the crystal ball has shown you all the images you need and you have shared them, they will begin to fade. Don't just stop the session suddenly; instead reverse the process you used at the beginning. Visualise the mists coming back and covering the images, then receding to return the ball to its natural state."

"Thank your crystal ball for the reading and put it away carefully." As to this last part I commented to Mr. Houdini "how facetious" "I agree Mrs. Watson the crystal ball is after all merely a stage prop in a performance and nothing more it processes no special powers or abilities…but like any great and convincing performance *thanking it* for its service is just a part of the act."

Marie of course did not have any knowledge that the medium she was soliciting help from already knew through extensive investigation by her co-conspirators the answers to all the questions that would be asked that afternoon and many afternoons to follow…on the other hand Marie had been suitably impressed and somewhat satisfied with the events that had unfolded in aiding her to reach and contact a man who had been suddenly taken from her life…and did not have the privilege of saying a final good bye to.

As if to indicate to Marie that the first (of many) readings had ended Ashley placed the white silk handkerchief back over the crystal ball then silently started to rise from her chair.

When Marie followed suite both walked towards the parlour door. When they covered the short distance together Ashley commented to Marie "You do know your way back to the street entrance?" Standing at the threshold Ashley could begin to sense Marie's uncertainty about ever returning.

To stem this potential loss the medium sought to assure Marie with "Miss Hinson with the skills and abilities I employ the events and memories I try to discover have none of the absolute certainty as say reading ones horoscope each day in the newspaper would have...there are many factors and forces that influence any outcome...only with much time and patience will the questions in your heart be answered and your spirit will be at peace."

Chapter 19

The next morning with Peter off to his place of employment in the city Sherlock, Alice and I were sitting at the kitchen table of 156 East Forsyth Street, Sunnyside Gardens finishing our second cup of breakfast coffee...a beverage I had only recently discovered and had come to enjoy. While sharing with Alice the events that had taken place the previous evening at dinner at the Houdini residence Sherlock and I had begun to look at the recent information as part of some large and unsolved jig saw puzzle.

I wasn't too long until we three together began to metaphorically put all of the pieces on the table and by turning over, trying to arrange and rearrange each piece to connect how all the information we had learned about the Houdini's niece fitted in with what Sherlock and I already knew and were learning about Miss Taggart.

When we had (in a manner of speaking) completed the outline of our puzzle we realized we were going to require more information. "And because" Sherlock sagely observed "Miss Taggart would no doubt recognize Mary from their previous encounters and would certainly question why a man would seek out her help we shall have to employ someone else to undertake this task that she has no knowledge of."

Pausing for a second then asking "Mrs. Eastman" Sherlock now turned to my cousin to give her his full attention "it would be of great help if you could without any subterfuge on your part assist us finding out what you can about Miss Taggart's new criminal venture?"

The plan we arrived at was for Alice and I to take a taxicab to 141 Wooster St. Apt. 4 d in Greenwich Village where we would part company for a time and she would go to make general inquiries about seeking help from the medium. Sherlock, in a separate taxicab would travel to the New York Public Library located on Fifth Avenue at its intersection with 42nd Street. There he would spend the day in the Rose Main Reading Room.

From what he shared about the library at dinner that evening we were told that the main reading room is a majestic 78 feet wide and 297 feet long, with 52-foot high ceilings. It is lined with thousands of reference works on open shelves along the floor level and along the balcony, lit by massive windows, grand chandeliers, and furnished with sturdy wood tables, comfortable chairs, and green shaded brass desk lamps.

Readers study books brought to them from the library's closed stacks...it would be here that Sherlock would find out about the dubious history and of the world of mediums and spiritualists in New York City.

Chapter 20

Sherlock exited from the taxicab...paid his fare then made his way from the busy pedestrian sidewalk up the short flight of stairs of the 42nd street entrance past the two imposing sculptured stone lions each guarding the entry and went into the incandescent lit interior of the New York Public Library.

He quickly crossed the cream coloured marble tiled floor and vaulted ceiling foyer (slightly echoing his footsteps) to reach the broad and imposing main staircase where he briskly climbed the two flights of stairs until reaching the third floor. At the top of the stairs directly ahead of him was his destination...being room 315 the Library's famous Rose Main Reading Room

Entering the hushed cathedral like atmosphere of the book lined and carpeted room (which he noted had the subtle back ground scent of ancient resting tomes) Sherlock surveying all that was around him could see that most of the study desks in the room were already in use so before approaching the reference librarian's desk with his request.

To claim a desk he removed his cap and gently placed it on one of the few remaining unoccupied ones whose green shaded brass desk lamp had not yet been lit.

Almost reverently approaching the reference librarian he noticed that her focus was engaged in an activity of stamping library cards and returning each to its pocket in the back of the book it was associated with.

Before engaging her he made note of the reference librarian's name from the small brass name plate located on the desk in front of her...it was E. Williams. She was familiarly known to her family and close friends as Bessie...an English diminutive of Elizabeth

"Miss Williams?" Sherlock started in a voice that he hoped was just audible enough to draw her attention away from the task she was involved with...but not distracting enough to disturb the other persons in the room.

Hearing her name spoken in a distinctive male voice but not acknowledging the speaker right away the reference librarian put the stamp she had been employing down on the desk...inserted the last card in its pocket...closed the book then looked up at Sherlock.

She studied the man standing before her for a minute as if to assess from his character and attire his purpose for attracting her attention then inquired in a primary school teacher's voice and tone she thought appropriate for the situation "May I be of assistance?"

The person addressing Sherlock from the other side of desk...I was told later...was probably in her mid to late 50's and from her general appearance and manner he took her to be a spinster.

As if describing a suspect in a case he might be engaged in Sherlock listed her physical characteristics as Chestnut hair with just a touch of grey styled in a fashion that might be taken from an earlier time...horn rim glasses framing clear azure blue intelligent eyes ...a face and facial features that reflected her apparent age...but at the same time somehow ageless...and as she was seated at the time Sherlock described that she was wearing a plain white linen blouse (buttoned at the collar)...the only decorative item on her person was a gold nurses watch pinned on the left side.

It was when she later arose from her desk to assist him that the blouse was accompanied by a sombre knee length plain grey woolen skirt matched with sensible black leather shoes.

Not too sure if the reference librarian had any knowledge of him...or even as to how she would react to his somewhat unusual request Sherlock confidently stated "With certain recent events coming to pass I wish to conduct research on the nature and practises concerning mediums and spiritualists in New York City."

Expecting to be dismissed with a cold and condescending "you must be joking...please do not waste my time with such foolishness the reference librarian instead stood up from her desk and asked with genuine interest "where are you seated Mr.?" "Holmes" he quickly returned

As they approached the study desk Sherlock had earlier claimed with his cap the reference librarian gave Sherlock some much needed instruction "Approaching the paranormal...Mr. Holmes...from any perspective is often difficult because of the lack of acceptable physical evidence from most of the purported phenomena.

By definition, the paranormal does not conform to conventional expectations of nature. Therefore, a phenomenon cannot be confirmed as paranormal using the scientific method because, if it could be, it would no longer fit the definition.

However, confirmation would result in the phenomenon being reclassified as part of science. Despite this problem, studies on the paranormal are periodically conducted by researchers from various disciplines.

Some researchers simply study the beliefs in the paranormal regardless of whether the phenomena are considered to objectively exist. Sherlock answered "In solving a problem of this sort Miss Williams, the grand thing is to be able to reason backward."

Respectably regarding Sherlock as she would any other person making a request the reference librarian finished with "I agree...if you will excuse me I will gather the relevant research books that may be of some assistance to you...is there anything else you require?"

Sherlock thought to himself and realized the answers he sought after might not all be contained in the books that would shortly be delivered to him. "Does the library archive back issues of the news papers published in and around New York City?"

Without any hesitation she answered "while our collection is comprehensive it only extends back for 6 months from the current date...which news papers and dates are you interested in looking at?"

Not quite believing his good fortune he answered "the daily newspapers, including the tabloid papers...if possible and" here he stopped and as if doing a mathematics problem in his head "three months back from today's date?"

Chapter 21

Sherlock occupied most of his the day in the literary sanctuary pouring through an initially small but growing mountain of reference books and back issues of New York City news papers.

Eagerly recording what he read thus adding to the knowledge about spiritualists and mediums he had previously acquired from his time spent with Harry Houdini.

Among his finds there was…Leonore Piper perhaps the greatest American medium ever one of the most spectacular and outstanding mental mediums who ever lived. No one, not even the most hardened closed minded skeptic after investigating her mediumship had ever suggested fraud.

She was able to convert the greatest materialist, closed minded skeptic this world has ever seen - Richard Hodgson. Because of her brilliant accurate information, Hodgson, who was contracted to by the British Society for Psychical Research engaged private detectives to follow her, to report on whom she met outside her home, to intercept her mail, to invite negative 'dummy' sitters unknown to anyone to her sittings - and to do everything possible to prove that this highly gifted brilliant American was not genuine. All failed and she remained the greatest American mental medium who triumphed over great challenges.

Another was Arthur Ford an American Spiritualist medium and founder of the International General Assembly of Spiritualists. Ford realized his psychic abilities during World War I. While in the army he would "hear" the names of people he served with, and those names would appear on the casualty lists several days later.

In the years after the war he investigated psychic phenomena and eventually joined the Spiritualists. Around 1921 Ford emerged as a trance medium, and "Fletcher," his control for the rest of his life, made his first appearance in trance sessions. He developed a popular following and traveled to Great Britain.

One of his lectures was attended by a veteran Spiritualist and famous English detective novel author, who enthusiastically told people the next day, "One of the most amazing things I have ever seen in years of psychic experience was the demonstration of Arthur Ford."

Betty White the wife of Stewart Edward White. In 1922 Betty discovered, while using a Ouija board, that she was able to communicate with entities which would later be dubbed "the invisibles". They invited a small circle of friends including "Darby and Joan" to participate in sessions during which her channelling abilities matured. Stewart's first book openly acknowledging Betty's contacts was *The Betty Book* a compilation of the messages his wife received followed shortly thereafter by *Across the Unknown*.

These first books resulted in thousands of letters from the readers. The White's were very private people who had kept Betty's abilities under wraps for over a decade.

Stewart Edward White was an author who published a number of books of "channelled" material. He studied at the University of Michigan (Ph.D., 1895; M.A., 1903).

In 1904 he married Elizabeth (Betty) Grant, and they settled in California where he became well known as an author of many books, articles, and short stories dealing with his experiences around the state in mining and lumber camps, and on exploration trips. He wrote *The Betty Book, Gaelic Manuscripts, The Road I Know , The Stars Are Still There , and (his most popular metaphysical work) and With Folded Wings* .

And in a Niagara Falls New York newspaper Sherlock read an interesting motion picture review:

Is Spiritualism a Fraud? (also known as : The Medium Exposed) is a 1906 British short drama film, directed by Walter R. Booth (also credited to J.H. Martin), featuring a medium exposed as a fake during a séance. The trick film is, "one of the last films made by R.W. Paul in collaboration with the trick-film specialist W.R. Booth," and according to Michael Brooke of British Film Institute, "combines elements of the previous year's The Unfortunate Policeman with a special effects sequence. However, unlike Booth and Paul's other work, here the mechanisms are deliberately revealed," "the crucial difference between his illusions and those of a medium is that Booth's audience knew that they were being deceived, but were happy to go along with the charade for the sake of both entertainment and the pleasure of working out how it was done."

When Sherlock had finished his research he straightened the accumulated collection of research books and newspapers that the reference librarian had provided him throughout his time at the reading room.

Turning off the deck lamp to indicate that this desk was now free for others to use he put his cloth cap back on his head and proceeded to Miss William's desk to thank her for her assistance.

"Have you been successful in your research on the nature and practises concerning mediums and spiritualists in New York City Mr. Holmes?" A brief smile played across Sherlock's face

"When one has a knock at the door Miss Williams, one does not pause, but goes further to see what causes it and investigates, and sooner or later and goes to discover if a message is believed to be delivered.

So I have gone to investigate the knocks, but as a result of my efforts I must confess that I am farther than ever from belief in the genuineness of Spirit manifestations and after my time here conducting research and endeavor I declare that nothing has been revealed to convince me that intercommunication has or ever could be established between the Spirits of the departed and those still in the flesh."

Chapter 22

Alice composed herself to face the uncertain then pushed the small black door buzzer button that was located just below a small brass framed name card that revealed the occupant of apt 4d as only "A Taggart".

Not hearing any corresponding sound of a buzzer or feet lightly treading down the stairs to answer Alice was about to leave when she saw the street entrance door to 141 Wooster Street open inward and there in person standing in the door way was the young lady I had described encountering in Gravesend, London and now possibly in Central Park.

Ashley momentarily displayed to Alice an expression which indicated she was not happy about this unplanned interruption in her day...and just for a second coldly gazed at her...then switching to a look of feigned interest (a skill she had much practise at) then politely asked "may I help you?"

Alice would share with me later during our planned late lunch at Henry's (a small outdoor café located at 42nd Street and Broadway, at the southeast corner of Times Square) that among her brief observations about the medium Alice had found herself wordless because as she looked into Ashley's dark soulless almost bottomless eyes she found that she was unable to speak.

Still transfixed Alice silently reached into her hand bag and retrieved a news paper advertisement similar to the one that had first brought Marie to the mediums attention. Ashley took the piece of paper from Alice's hand…looked at it and started to read…

"Are you searching for peace of mind…answers to unresolved questions…does happiness and joy elude you? As an experienced spiritual medium I have the answers you seek and I can help to find whatever you are seeking…the past present and future revealed…telephone Bry (for the Bryant telephone exchange) 2424 for an appointment." she finished reading the advertisement and closely scrutinized Alice…then like a feral black cat that has sensed it might somehow be in danger or has perceived something dangerous to itself…as only black cats can Ashley felt the hair on the back of her neck to start to prickle.

Ashley handed to advertisement back to Alice…all the while trying to think that she might have seen this woman standing in front of her somewhere before. "What are you seeking?" she asked cautiously but still intrigued that this person might possibly represent a new source of easy income.

Alice fumbling for an answer flashed back to our morning meal then replied "I…I" she stammered then continued "I certainly do not wish to contact a departed loved one". Here Alice stopped momentarily to gauge Ashley's reaction to this leading statement hoping it might reveal some detail of what was taking place between the medium and Marie.

All Alice received in turn from this failed deception was an annoyed look from Ashley that conveyed the thought of "my time is valuable…so please do not waste any more of it."

Alice continued on with the second request she and I had also rehearsed together at breakfast. As convincingly as she could she resumed with "My husband has not received a raise in pay from his employer for some time and he wants to know if he should address this matter or perhaps seek another position."

Ashley hearing the jaws of a trap that Alice had tried to set snap shut without capturing her coolly but not too convincingly replied "I may be of assistance to you"…here she paused for a moment to silently let Alice know she hadn't really accepted either request as being convincing…"and to your husband concerning his present or future employment prospects.

I will see you at this time and day next week where we shall discuss this matter in a more private setting."

Just as she was to ascend the stairs and return to her apartment Ashley stopped…turned around and looked directly at Alice then commented "I didn't catch your last name"

My cousin realized she hadn't given it when they had first met with but from the mediums likely reputation she probably already had knowledge of it. With what she was about to revel Alice knew that Ashley would soon no doubt connect her to me and maybe even to Sherlock (making the brief meeting between them their first and certainly their last) Alice confidently answered "Eastman…Mrs. Alice Eastman."

Chapter 23

As with her first visit Marie again found herself again standing at the street entrance to 141 Wooster Street wondering that if she should push the small black door buzzer button for apt 4d...and while standing there asking herself if perhaps by performing this small action she could start the process to healing the deep wound in her heart and at last find some measure of closure.

Looking first at the door then the buzzer she started hearing two conflicting voices in her mind each demanding attention and each insisting on following a separate and conflicting action.

To stop them both from battling any further she said in a low voice to herself "silence!" then pushed the button and waited for the medium to come down the stairs to open the door and welcome her in. When the door opened inward Marie was greeted with "Miss Hinson how nice to see you again"

Accompanied up the stairs by Ashley...when both reached the landing Marie found she was again crossing a familiar threshold...entering a familiar parlour...and being silently directed to sit in the same chair she had sat in during her last visit.

After becoming comfortable Marie observed Ashley...as before walk away from the table...go and close the parlour door only this time it was done in a curious manor as if she was trying to prevent someone or something threatening from entering the room. When the task was completed Ashley then returned and took her seat on the other side of the small clothed covered round table.

The medium sat silently not saying anything for a minute then slowly closed her eyes and gently placed her hands on the still covered crystal ball as if perhaps to begin meditating or clearing her mind before starting the reading.

With the medium apparently going deep into thought Marie furtively looked about the room to see if anything had been added or removed from her last visit that might give some slight hint about the person in front of her...the one she would soon entrust her feelings...emotions and now money to.

She found her attention drawn back to the medium sized brass floor lamp (along with the table and chairs being the only furniture in the room) still standing silent guard in an opposite corner of the parlour.

She was still curious about the large cream hued circular shaped lamp shade which to her had appeared to be oriental in nature because it was decorated with bright water color paints as if to perhaps illustrate some exotic story...and perhaps by asking the medium about it might reveal a clue about herself or her personality.

Just as she started ask she saw that the medium was still in some sort of mystical trance Marie found herself going back again to the lamp and getting lost in imagining what that exotic story might be when she heard the barely audible sound of Ashley gently clearing her throat to attract Marie's attention back to the table.

When Marie met Ashley's full gaze she felt a deep chill run through her that one should only expect to experience on a bitter and freezing winter morning while standing on an open railway platform while waiting for the train to take you into the city and not on warm summer day like today.

Ashley fixed her full attention on the person sitting on the other side of the table then asked "Before we begin Miss Hinson...I have a question to ask you...do you know of any one named Alice Eastman?"

Chapter 24

By the time Alice had arrived at Henry's most of the lunch hour regulars had already finished their midday meal and were now getting up and leaving the establishment to return to their places of employment or business.

As she was entering the much quieter....less occupied cafe and while making her way past the now mostly empty tables to the one I was sitting at I tried to surmise from her presence and appearance just how the meeting had transpired between her and Ashley.

First sitting down in the opposite chair facing mine I saw a bemused smile momentarily play across her face and in place of the customary salutation of "hello" I was curiously greeted with "Have you ordered lunch yet?" Caught off guard I automatically replied "No" and then focussing on her almost blank expression I found myself enquiring "did you see and talk to Miss Taggart?"

Alice in the midst of unbuttoning her coat stopped for a moment to replay in her mind the event that had transpired earlier in Greenwich Village then answered my question with "not so much talk Mary...I just found that when she looked at me I was unable to speak."

Regaining her composure while finishing the task she had started she continued "I did however present her with the newspaper advertisement and asked the questions you and I had rehearsed together at breakfast...but somehow but I think she saw through me because she quickly answered me with a rather cold..."*I may be of assistance to you and to your husband concerning his present or future employment prospects. I will see you at this time and day next week where we shall discuss this matter in a more private setting."*

During lunch we both came to the realization that this limited avenue of investigation could no longer be pursued and was now closed.

It would be up to Sherlock and I, possibly the Houdini's and to some degree the Eastman's to find out with what we had all learned and what the connection was between the Houdini's niece and the newly minted (in my mind anyway) medium...and more importantly what the medium hoped to gain from her new client.

Chapter 25

Marie felt compelled to quickly search through every corner of her mind to see if she in some way had any connection to the name the medium had pointedly asked her about.

Fearing that is she had even scant knowledge it could jeopardise her connection. She thought perhaps that her famous uncle or aunt might know the name...but she could not recollect a time when this Alice Eastman's name had ever come up in conversation.

Feeling that in spite of giving the answer she knew was true she wondered if the medium in fact believed her when Marie shook her head with what she hoped was a convincing *no*.

Ashley gazed at her for a minute...again removing a white silk handkerchief from a now familiar object on the table sitting between them. Marie gazed again at the large crystal ball that was nestled in its delicate and ornate pewter cradle as if the transparent orb held all the answers.

Having already created the proper mood and atmosphere Ashley laid her hands gently on the crystal ball for a minute or two in order to give the appearance of energizing and strengthening her psychic rapport with it.

While holding the crystal ball Ashley ran through all the information in her mind (like a meticulous accountant going over a ledger) that had been gathered about the now deceased Trevyn James Craddock and felt confident she would be ready to answer any question Marie might ask.

The medium removed her hands from the crystal ball....appeared to stare deeply in to it and Marie was sure the mediums eyes had started to relax and become slightly unfocussed.

With what had transpired in front of her so far Marie was almost convinced that there was some sort of mist or smoke forming in the crystal ball and that the medium was allowing this mist to grow and fill the ball, then visualising it gradually clearing to reveal anticipated images within the sphere."

While still very focused on the crystal ball Ashley's voice barely audible said "The images that I am passing onto you from the crystal ball may not be what you expected.

That's OK, don't fight them. Your subconscious mind knows what information you need. Just let the images I present to you flow, changing and taking you wherever they choose to go. Don't try to rationalise them now, there will be time for that later."

For the better part of the hour Ashley "shared" the supposed images the crystal ball was revealing giving Marie tantalizing but frustratingly brief glimpses of things she desired to know.

Then just when the medium knew that she had piqued Marie's interest and while still gazing deep into the crystal ball she calmly announced "The crystal ball has shown you and shared with you all the images you need to know right now."

"But" Marie plaintively started. Ashley looked up from the imagined depths of the crystal ball and back to the anxious young lady sitting on the other side of the small round cloth covered table then coldly closed the matter with "Once the crystal ball has shown you all the images you need and I have shared them, they will begin to fade. The mists that proceeded the images return and cover them then the crystal ball returns to its natural state."

Two final events that unfolded told Marie that her time with the medium had ended...first Ashley covered the crystal ball...then she silently rose from her chair and started towards the parlour door indicating that Marie without questioning was to do the same.

Her final words to her now very bewildered and confused client at the threshold were "I will see you at this same day and time next week." Not waiting for any acknowledgment or response...Ashley turned and went back into to her parlour.

Chapter 26

Taking in and appreciating the remarkable atmosphere of reading room and the impressive amount of information it contained within its walls one last time.

Sherlock now with the information in hand he had been seeking turned and retraced his steps from the morning to make his way back down the stair case then across the foyer and again pass the two imposing sculptured stone lions each still guarding the 42nd street entrance of the New York City Library.

In the late afternoon sun he crossed the sidewalk to the curb passing through the sparse pedestrian traffic and with new found confidence raised his right hand into the busy and still noisy traffic where he hailed a taxicab that would return him to the Eastman's residence.

Supper that night was as much about sharing an enjoyable evening meal together as it was collating the information that Sherlock, Alice and I had individually gathered about Ashley Laurinda Taggart pickpocket, abductor, kidnapper and now apparently amateur medium.

Sherlock finishing the last of his meal then looked at each of us in turn and announced "with what we already know about Miss Taggarts criminal activities in England and with the little we know to date about her activities in New York City I think it would be wise at this point to involve Mr. And Mrs. Houdini by sharing what we here have learned.."

As if to give us a direction to go in Sherlock continued "Perhaps by pursuing this course of action" here he stopped and I could hear the conviction in his voice drop a little "they...with our help may be able to persuade their niece Marie to not make any further visits to the medium and ease their concern about her.

Sherlock paused...then continued with that the conviction dropped a little more "however in the event that they are unsuccessful...with Mr. Houdini's considerable experience in exposing mediums it might be possible that in some way Miss Taggart will be caught out and rather than continuing in her new career in New York will find herself instead making the return trip to Southampton in the custody of Mrs. Watson and myself."

I thought that at the time that this would be the most practical approach to take and felt that all at the table were in favor of first contacting the Houdini's before proceeding with any alternative plan.

The one thing I remember about that particular meal was Peter's almost imperceptible and odd reaction to Sherlock's seemingly logical suggestion. A moment later and it had vanished and rising from the table he announced "I'll call the Houdini's and invite them over tomorrow night."

Chapter 27

With each appointment attended in Greenwich Village Marie felt as if she was getting further and further away from the original reason she had desperately reached out to Ashley for help in the first place and more and more like she was sinking into some sort of spiritual quicksand that she might not be able to escape from.

Marie had felt a certain sense of shameful pride in that she had been able to keep (or hide) these visits from friends and co workers.

But with in her there was a growing conflict because she could not reveal or explain to her uncle and aunt the grounds for...much less the motivation as to the continued visits to the medium knowing what her uncle thought of them. She had come to suspect that her uncle and aunt had some knowledge of her coming and going but could not summon the courage to bring the subject up.

The first time she had ever experienced feelings similar to this was when she was about nine years old and had run away from her uncles and aunts home. She had never been to a five-and-dime store (a five and dime is a store that sells a variety of inexpensive household items at discounted prices.

The name refers to a category of stores that became popular in the late 19th century), so one day they had taken her. They walked there from 113th Street to 25th Street, and she looked and saw things there for nickel and for a dime. They bought her a little something, and she didn't even remember what it was.

A few days later, or the following day, her mother was going to come pick Marie up to take her home. She wanted to buy presents, but didn't have any money. So she conned them (her uncle and aunt). First, she went to her aunt and said, "Do you think you could give me a nickel or a dime so that I could buy my mother a present?"

Before you know it, she gave her a nickel. Marie remembers that she thinks she wound up with about fifty cents. At that time, nobody could take her [to the store]...they were going to have a dinner party. Her aunt couldn't take her...her uncle couldn't take her, and nobody could take her. Marie was heartbroken and remembers sitting up in her room by herself. She thought, "I know how to walk there. It's just straight blocks. I'm going to go there myself."

She doesn't remember what dress she had on, but had put on her Sunday black patent leather shoes. She didn't tell anybody, and left with a little purse that had the money in. So on the way, it started to rain, so she took her shoes and socks off and put them under her arm. She walked through every puddle and had a grand time. When she got to the five-and-ten, she went around buying presents. She bought perfume and all different things, and spent her fifty cents.

All of a sudden, they realized on 113th Street [Houdini's home] that Marie was missing. Well, her uncle yelled "Marie!" and when they couldn't find her really, they got hysterical. Marie didn't realize how long it would take her, and that she spent a lot of time at the store.

Houdini sent word out to his people...that his niece was missing. [The police] had horses and they didn't have police cars...so in the store, a policeman came up to her and said "What's your name?" she said, "Marie." He said, "Do you have an Uncle Harry?" and she said "Oh yes. My uncle is Uncle Harry. I'm his niece."

So he said, "Will you come with us? We're going to take you back. He's very worried about you." They put her on top of the horse.

Marie was delighted. She had never been on a horse in her life. So all of a sudden, they get back to 113th Street, and there was a crowd of people, and her uncle was in the middle. When he saw her, the tears were running down his face. She on the other hand was having a grand time.

He said to her, "When I get you inside, I'm going to kill you." Well, she only laughed harder. When he got her inside, he said "Do you know how scared I was? I thought somebody ran away with you." She had emerald green eyes and dark auburn hair, so he said, "Everybody wants to have somebody with green eyes and auburn hair." And she believed him, so never did it again.

Chapter 28

Alice Eastman (nee Hudson) had met her future husband Peter at the governor's (being Charles Seymour Whitman the 41st governor of New York) Christmas ball held at the New York State Executive Mansion in Albany on December 22, 1918.

She had been invited to attend by friends of her family. As Alice has always shared with me many times it was his smile to her that evening that she had seen from across the sea of elegantly dressed women and formally attired men during a Strauss waltz in the festively decorated chandelier lit ball room that had first attracted her to him.

Alice always blushes a little when she tells of how Peter had surprised her by proposing marriage while they on an ice skating date together with other couples one cold winter Friday afternoon on the reservoir in Central Park.

She sometimes wonders if it was chance, coincidence or planned because it also happened to be Valentine's Day February 14, 1919 when this wonderful event took place.

Just after he had asked her it had started to lightly snow and she remembers that she didn't even need to think about his romantic request when at that moment the world and the snowflakes seemed (for her) to pause...for a just second then continued to gently fall when she had replied "yes".

It had been a proper courtship and engagement in which they had got to know, appreciate and be comfortable with each other as well as giving time for her family (the Hudson's) and his family (the Eastman's) to become acquainted and familiar with each other.

Alice and Peter were married at a civil ceremony in September of that year (just as the leaves were staring to turn to their autumn colors) and moved (she from the family home...he from a cold water walk up apartment) to their present home shortly after the honeymoon.

Domestic life for both had comfortably settled with Peter going into the city each day to practice law while Alice tended to the house in the morning then spent the afternoon going out to volunteer with or participate at a number of charitable organizations or societies depending on the day of the week it was.

Although Alice had known that her charming young man, suitor, fiancé and now husband was a lawyer and that he practiced entertainment law (in matters concerning actors and performers) with a small law firm. She was never really curious or interested enough about the details of her husband's employment to ask more than a few superficial questions when the matter had first come up in conversation.

Archer & Greiner P.C. (personal and confidential)....the firm who employed Peter is located in a city block bounded by 42nd Street, 8th Avenue, 41st Street, and 7th Avenue. They have a modest client base that includes several well known stage and film actors, musician's escape artists and magicians. Known to only a close few in the law firm it quietly looks after the legal interests of one or two famous and powerful spiritualists and mediums.

Chapter 29

Peter had planned to be home well ahead of his invited guest's arrival in an attempt to subtly take the pulse of the evening and not feel he may be excluded from any privileged conversation that might be of interest to him.

But due to a last minute just before closing visit at the law office by one of his more important clients (who had claimed it was an urgent matter) had meant that Peter's commuter train ride home would leave Pen Station an hour later from his usual departure time.

At 156 East Forsyth Street, Sunnyside Gardens Manhattan as I was adding the finishing touches to the simmering beef stew that was to be the evening meal Alice had brought out and was spreading a new white linen table cloth over an extended kitchen table.

After smoothing it with her hands (to remove any creases) she set about creating...with her good china and silver wear...instead of the accustomed four dinner places she was now setting six places for supper

As she was making last minute adjustments to the individual place settings there was a knock at the front door. Looking back over her shoulder in my direction she asked "Mary can you go to see who is...I believe it will be the Houdini's."

Putting the wooden stirring spoon I had been using down on the counter beside me I left the kitchen and Alice at her task then made my way to the front hall way

Turning the door knob and opening the front door inward there standing before me on the spacious covered ground level veranda framed by an evening street scene were two faces and forms I had remembered both from the Hippodrome Theater and from an interesting dinner at their home.

"Mr. Houdini...Mrs. Houdini" I greeted them both cordially and continued "a pleasure to see you both again." Harry Houdini beamed and returned the greeting with "the pleasure is also mine." Bess Houdini in her soft voice also replied "it is good to see you again Mrs. Watson."

There was that pause in the conversation between us that always follows introductions when nobody seems to know quite what to say next. Catching a look of puzzlement that momentarily played over Harry Houdini's face I answered the unasked (where is?) question.

"Alice is in the kitchen setting the table and keeping an eye on our supper...Sherlock is in his guest room going over some information he brought back from the library. Peter has not returned home yet. But please come in and make yourselves comfortable and I will let Alice and Sherlock know you are both here."

Leading them both into the Eastman's home I took their coats and hats to hang up and at the same time directed the arrived guests into the comfortably furnished parlour.

Leaving the Houdini's to choose where they both wanted to be seated I hung up their outer wear and first returned to the kitchen and announced their arrival to Alice...then made my way to Sherlock's guest room door.

Knocking softly...I heard from within the room a familiar polite response of "yes" I replied "it's me Sherlock I just wanted you to know that the Houdini's have arrived." With that I heard him rise from where he had been seated then heard his footsteps making their way to the door.

Opening it fully he looked knowingly at me and said "and so Mary it begins." As if to assure himself somehow that all the participants in this matter would be present he questioned "has Mr. Eastman returned home from work yet?"

"He should be returning shortly" was my semi certain answer to his inquiry ..."Alice tells me that some nights he is home at this time and other nights some matter comes up with his work...requiring his attention then he arrives home a bit later."

"Well then" Sherlock announced as he switched off his guest room light (with his right hand) and closed the door behind him "we shall all engage in social pleasantries until Mr. Eastman's return" and together we both made our way to the parlour.

Chapter 30

Joining the others already seated in the room we were all doing our best to make and maintain polite small talk yet all the while carefully trying to avoid the subject (of Marie) that had all brought us to this one place.

When the well of conversation had almost gone dry all of us had our attention drawn to the front door as we heard it opening and witnessed Peter make what appeared to be a somewhat rushed entrance.

Alice got up first from where she had been seated and preceded to her husband with a mixture of happiness and relief that he was now home and at the same time concern for his apparent state.

Helping him to remove his coat while he placed his brief case on a small table in the front hall ...Alice first tried to read her husband's mood...but any reason for his rushed entrance had in an instant vanished from his face.

Displaying genteel martial affection towards her husband...Alice drew him into the parlour...then he apologized to all present for his lateness.

There was a pause that left us not knowing how to or if we should reply to the apology…to break the growing uncomfortable silence Alice enthusiastically announced "if we are ready let us go into the kitchen for supper."

While moving kitchen chairs (out from and then back to the table) and sorting out as to who would sit next to who during the meal at the finely set table Alice made her way to the stove (range) to transfer the warm and delicious smelling stew from the pot where it had been slowly and aromatically simmering in all day into a large white porcelain serving bowl.

 All eyes were fixed on her as the filled bowl (and serving ladle) with its warm steaming delicious contents was placed in the middle of the table next to a tray containing an already sliced loaf of home baked white bread and butter dish.

Alice took her seat... she looked around at all at the table…then slightly lifting the serving ladle in Harry Houdini's direction said "Mr. Houdini…would you do Mary and me the honor of being the first to try the meal?"

"It would be my pleasure" he replied then started to serve himself…but he knew before continuing that Alice and I were waiting for his opinion so he sampled the meal…he paused…smiled and commented to both of us "excellent!"

He finished helping himself and asked to have bread and butter passed to him. The serving bowl, bread and butter then made the circuit around the table...it was passed first left to his wife...then to me...to Sherlock...to Peter and finally to Alice.

Unlike the lively and sparkling back and forth conversation Sherlock and I had enjoyed in the company of the Eastman's on our first evening in New York City at the Russian tea room this meal was more as if all at supper had taken some vow of silence and had decided on having only their thoughts for company. The hushed atmosphere at the table was only occasionally disturbed by dinner related requests.

With some interest I had noticed that Sherlock was the only one at the table who did not have a second helping of the evening meal.

Instead when he had finished he had carefully placed his fork and knife on the plate in front of him then sat in contemplative silence while watching and waiting for the others around him to finish the last of their meal.

As each finished they in turn realized that Sherlock...from his pose now required their attention. When the last fork and knife was laid on its respective plate Sherlock raised an eye brow in appreciation and started.

"Compulsion...a noun...as defined in Webster's dictionary is an irresistible impulse to perform some act. Your niece Miss Marie Hinson...Mr. and Mrs. Houdini...from what Mrs. Eastman, Mrs. Watson and I have learned is under some compulsion to make regular visits to a medium located in Greenwich Village."

"While we are moving blind on this I feel certain though that Miss Hinson's decision may have been motivated by some emotional distress this is a common theme between mediums and their clients.

If this proves to be true it means that your niece is very vulnerable to whatever unscrupulous schemes or traps that the medium may have already set for her."

"As to the method your niece employed to seek this help I believe it was by way of an advertisement located in the back pages of a New York tabloid paper.

However the method there are two facts we are certain of...first that the young lady your niece goes to visit with is no more a medium than any one of us here tonight is. Her name is Ashley Laurinda Taggart and before coming to New York City she had been living with her family above a butcher shop on Welbury Street in Hackney, that is a working class district in North London."

"Second...although presenting herself this time as a spiritual medium Miss Taggarts real talents lend themselves more to the criminal activities of pick pocketing, abduction and kidnapping.

These skills were employed against Mrs. Watson's writer friend who lives in Gravesend England. After being found out and eventually taken into custody for these crimes in a desperate bid to escape justice and incarceration Miss Taggart somehow found a way to escape and hurriedly depart from London to where she now resides.

As Mrs. Watson and I can attest to from the experience...is that the young lady has little or no conscience or morals and will stop at nothing to achieve whatever criminal goal she has set for herself."

Harry Houdini turned to his wife...took her hands in his...and for a moment they looked into each other's eyes searching for answers...but each face only reflected the look of helplessness the other was experiencing. Reaching for inner strength Harry Houdini broke his gaze to his wife...turned and looked to Sherlock then asked "What can we do Mr. Holmes?"

From the expression on his face I could tell that Sherlock wanted to give some careful thought before answering the poignant question. With all at the table waiting for a solution he calmly stated "I would suggest for the time being you and Mrs. Houdini take a simple approach.

When the time is right...ask your niece about this matter...what made her decide to follow the path she has chosen...offer her whatever help and support you both can. Then perhaps try to advise her of the risks she will certainly be taking if she continues with the visits."

With those comforting words of advice being spoken the hushed atmosphere that had descended at the start of the meal had dissipated much the same way a morning fog dissipates as the sun rises to make it melt away.

Soon the sound of friendly conversation filled the Eastman's kitchen as Alice and I removed the dishes, utensils serving bowl and tray from the table that had made an otherwise subdued dinner still enjoyable.

The conversation then moved from the kitchen table back to the Eastman's comfortable parlour. For the next while Harry Houdini shared with us some of the world stages he and his wife had performed on...and without divulging any secrets some of the amazing illusions and escapes he with his wife's assistance had performed.

As the hour was growing late...Harry Houdini rose from where he had been seated...reached for his wife's hand to help her rise and announced to all present that it was time for them both to be returning home.

On cue the rest of us arose and escorted our guests to the front hall where Peter handed Harry Houdini his coat and Alice handed Bess Houdini her coat.

Saying our final collective goodbyes to our hopefully relieved guests Alice closed the front door...turned and announced to Sherlock and I..."Peter and I are going to retire to our room...so we will say good night to you Mary and to you also Mr. Holmes."

As Peter was making his way to their bed room...and Sherlock was also making his way to his guest room...I gently put my hand on Alice's shoulder to stop her and draw her attention. She turned...acknowledged my gesture with a puzzled look and quizzically asked "yes Mary?"

Not sure if I was overstepping my family bounds as her cousin I...with some uncertainty asked "Is life with you and Peter going well?"

"What do you mean Mary?" Alice quickly and guardedly returned. Not quite sure where I was going with this line of thought...but with what I had witnessed tonight I continued.

Somehow knowing that she might quickly turn and go on the defensive I softened my approach to her with "I'm not sure" I saw in Alice's face the defensive attitude lower for a moment so I pressed on "When he returned home this evening Peter seemed...distant...preoccupied...a little withdrawn...cautious and maybe a bit guarded."

Alice stood silently in front of me for a moment...no doubt composing some positive "everything is alright" response she thought I wanted to hear.

I would have believed the next thing she was about to tell me...except that the smile she started with was the same one Miss Winifred Elizabeth Margaret Jeffrey had given me in a similar situation when she...like Alice was about to tell me words I wanted hear but not the truth.

Chapter 31

The residents of Wooster Street as well as any clients who had an appointment that morning with the medium residing upstairs in apartment 4 d of 141 were surprised to see a note fixed with a push pin just above the small brass framed name card that made known the name of the occupant dwelling there.

For those with any interest in the matter the hastily hand written (in pencil) note briefly explained that the tenet would be away for the morning on personal business (at a city block bounded by 42nd Street, 8th Avenue, 41st Street, and 7th Avenue) but would return early in the afternoon

---

Behind the closed office door an authoritative and booming male voice could be heard saying "Mr. Eastman...this situation has become quite intolerable" the source of the voice was a powerful, well known and famous spiritualist.

Peter watched with some trepidation as the tall stout...well attired and influential man slowly paced back and forth in front of him as if he was measuring the width of Peters desk.

"This would not be so bad...if only it was your wife who was involved. But we also have the great consulting detective Mr. Sherlock Holmes and with him the widow of Dr. Watson...Mary I believe is her name causing trouble."

"From what I have learned from my various sources is that since his arrival Mr. Holmes has been making good use of his time at the New York Public Library the one located on Fifth Avenue.

It has been learned he spent an afternoon conducting research in their famous reading room. Further from what I understand he was helped in his cause by a knowledgeable research librarian whose name I believe is Miss Elizabeth Williams."

"While this development may possibly be cause for some distress...with the right word placed here and there...much of what the research librarian has helped Mr. Holmes to discover.... what the great consulting detective himself knows with some certainty to be true and even for that matter much of what Mrs. Watson in her own way may have uncovered all of it could easily be dismissed as so much fabrication...hear say evidence...even to slanderous and libelous statements.

"Our greatest problem Mr. Eastman"...here the imposing client stopped pacing...turned and looked directly at Peter..."is one man....Harry Houdini.

I had hoped I would never have any direct involvement with him. He represents a real danger to us and also by professional association to you too.

So far any contact with him has been through words...sometimes heated and angry words... that may have been exchanged...in person when I have been performing on stage and also when he has.

Through much correspondence...and we have even employed the local newspapers through articles...columns and letters to the editor as our battlefronts."

"But up until now it has only been a harmless back and forth verbal exchange between us and nothing more...I wisely fear with Mr. Houdini's well-known feelings concerning my chosen calling and the help I offer that armed with the information he has acquired so far from all the parties concerned he will begin a crusade that will see me and others like me run out of town.

Chapter 32

"Please have a seat Miss Hinson" Ashley stated with a certain false charm as she directed Marie to sit in a now very familiar chair...across from a familiar table all set in an equally familiar parlour.

First looking down the medium lifted the white silk handkerchief away from the crystal ball then looked up at the person she was supposedly going tell her future to.

Although Ashley did not posses any real physic powers the working skills she had acquired in her new employment since coming to New York City told her that there was something on Marie's mind that might possibly jeopardise future lucrative visits.

Trying to sound both concerned and somewhat mystical Ashley gently probed the visible worry by stating "I sense you have come this afternoon with a matter that may be upsetting you."

In her mind Marie blurted out what was still upsetting her...that she was still coming to see Ashley and had not yet informed her aunt and uncle as to the where for or why...plus her growing frustration as to what was becoming to her increasingly pointless visits.

Even as she pondered Ashley's question...and how best to answer it Marie could feel a growing sense of dissatisfaction rising within her. As far as she could see to her and what she sought...all of this (as she took in everything that was immediately surrounding her) was like attempting to see the bottom of a small perfect round pool of clear rain water after it had been deliberately and repeatedly trod through...with big and heavy boots.

The careless action now creating a misshapen puddle that was opaque...murky and muddy...and never to be clear again...like the half answers and tantalizing but vague clues the medium was telling her about Trevyn James Craddock.

Sensing that giving the wrong answer to the medium could bring such little hope she had to an end Marie drew what small amount of resolve she had left inside herself...presented what she hoped was an untroubled smile...and answered Ashley "nothing serious...it's just that I had a disagreement with my friend Sarah at work the other day. I was hoping we could talk and mend our friendship."

With that the session began...as with so many times before Ashley drew on the information she had acquired from her associates about the young man while trying to disguise it as deep and spiritual messages.

And Marie with each word she heard from across the table felt as if she was standing at an open park in a gentle snow fall...trying to catch hold of and enfold each descending fragile flake that somehow in gently holding it close to her it might help ease her loss and at the same time keep that cold comfort from melting or falling to the ground.

Chapter 33

All of a sudden, they realized on 113th Street [Houdini's home] that Marie was missing. Well, her uncle yelled "Marie!" and when they couldn't find her really, they got hysterical. Marie didn't realize how long it would take her, and that she spent a lot of time at the store.

Houdini sent word out to his people...that his niece was missing. [The police] had horses and they didn't have police cars...so in the store, a policeman came up to her and said "What's your name?" she said, "Marie." He said, "Do you have an Uncle Harry?" and she said "Oh yes. My uncle is Uncle Harry. I'm his niece."

So he said, "Will you come with us? We're going to take you back. He's very worried about you." They put her on top of the horse. Marie was delighted. She had never been on a horse in her life. So all of a sudden, they get back to 113th Street, and there was a crowd of people, and her uncle was in the middle. When he saw her, the tears were running down his face. She on the other hand was having a grand time.

From the expression on his face I could tell that Sherlock wanted to give some careful thought before answering the poignant question. With all at the table waiting for a solution he calmly stated "I would suggest for the time being you and Mrs. Houdini take a simple approach...when the time is right...ask your niece about this matter...what made her decide to follow the path she has chosen...offer her whatever help and support you both can...then perhaps try to advise her of the risks she will certainly be taking if she continues with the visits."

Marie was surprised to see her Uncle Harry waiting for her at the employee's entrance of Beekman Paper and Card Company the business where she was employed as she was leaving to return to her home.

Momentarily caught off guard she still managed a cheery hello to her favorite relative..."Uncle Harry...what a nice surprise! What brings you all the way down here?" Harry Houdini in the same tone replied "I've come to collect my favorite niece to have dinner with me and her favorite aunt."

"Your aunt Bess and I haven't seen you in some time and wondered how you are getting along. Besides other than having some important guests over for dinner a short time ago it has just been her and I sitting together at a very large and empty table."

Realizing that her charming and persuasive uncle would not take no for an answer Marie putting on her coat agreed to the invitation and accompanied him home to a brownstone located at 278 W 113 Street in Harlem for a long overdue family meal.

As Harry Houdini and Marie walked through the front door Bess Houdini was already standing waiting to greet her niece. Marie wondered for a moment about the expression her on aunts face...to Marie her aunt looked like a sheppard that had found the lost lamb of the flock. Then silently taking her niece into her arms Marie felt safe and comfortable...like her aunt did not want to let her go.

Remembering Sherlock's suggestion Harry Houdini gently said to his wife "Come Bess I think that after a day at work Marie is hungry and would like to sit down to the meal you have prepared for us."

Leaving the parlour they entered the still warm, cozy and inviting dining room.   Marie looked around to familiarize herself with a part of the house she had not seen in some time then noticed that the table in anticipation of her arrival had been comfortably and intimately set for three.

Marie sitting down with her uncle...watched her aunt Bess make her way to the stove (range)...there with the help of thick oven mitts she in turn retrieved three plates of dinner from the oven that had been keeping each warm until Marie's arrival.

While any one observing this domestic scene would have only seen three family members sitting together enjoying the meal and each other's company...the furtive glances that passed between Harry Houdini and his wife when they thought Marie could not see them...spoke of an underlining tension of who would be first to broach the subject of Marie's state.

Realizing they had reached a momentary impasse Harry Houdini to dispel the silence that accompanied dinner filled the room with light conversation about general events that had taken place in his and Bess Houdini's life. When dinner was finished Bess Houdini asked her niece to help clear the table to make room for dessert.

While standing at the kitchen sink together scraping plates in preparation for them to be washed later Marie's aunt said to her niece in a low voice "Your uncle Harry would like to talk to you about something that concerns him."

Not sure as to what her uncle wanted to talk about...Marie returned to the table carrying three small plates of dessert. When her aunt sat down and handed out dessert spoons the last of the meal was also eaten in silence.

The stillness was finally broken when Bess Houdini rose from her chair and announced to her husband and niece "I have some things that need to be attend to...I will leave you and your uncle to talk."

When his wife exited the room Harry Houdini leaned forward a bit and looking sincerely into his nieces eyes gently said "Marie you know how much your aunt and I care about you and how much we love you."

Marie nodded her head in silent agreement..."and you know how much we worry about you." Marie knew this because she could still picture the look on her uncle's face as she (as a young girl) was being brought home on the back of a police horse.

Hoping some how he had started to open a door Harry Houdini waited for his niece to voluntarily begin...when instead all he saw on her face was a mixture of puzzlement and guarded hesitation so he continued.

"Your aunt and I believe that some sadness or unhappiness has come into your life and that it has possibly caused you some great sorrow." Like blindly feeling his way through a thick fog Harry Houdini continued..."this grief has left you with emptiness and many unanswered questions...but where you are presently seeking to find these answers...there will never be any real answers there.

Now the door was at last open and all his niece had to do is cross the threshold and the whole business of mediums...spiritualists and smoke filled crystal balls could easily be brought to an end.

Torn with how she knew she had to reply to the one person who meant the world to her...Marie heard herself saying to him as if she listening to an actress performing on stage "No Uncle Harry...if there is any sadness in my life right now it is because of the demands my employer is making on me and the other girls at work. There seems so much to do and not enough time to do it in."

Harry Houdini sat back in his chair and silently looked at his niece...watching the turmoil that was going on inside her he knew there was some compelling reason why she didn't want to tell him what he pretty much already knew.

As if to comfort the growing distress he could see in her troubled face...he leaned forward again and gently placed his hands gently on hers...with a loving voice told his nice "you know Aunt Bess and I will always be here for you...and we will respect any decisions you choose to make."

Chapter 34

On the concerned instructions of his wife...Harry Houdini called the Eastman residence and asked to speak to Sherlock. In the span of the brief telephone call it was arranged for the two to meet where they had first met and had become aquatinted.

Passing Sherlock as he was hanging up the receiver I gave him a quizzical look. Sherlock gave me one of his trade mark smiles and calmly answered "It seems that I have a return luncheon engagement with Mr. Houdini."

The next day at the appointed time and place Sherlock was standing out in front of number 80 Spring Street watching the people of New York City pass by in a steady parade when he saw one person break from the constantly moving stream of pedestrians and come towards him.

Not sure as to what had lead to this meeting...as his luncheon companion approached Sherlock offered him his hand and greeted him with a neutral "Hello Mr. Houdini."

While shaking Sherlock's hand Harry Houdini eagerly replied "I'm glad you could take the time to see me Mr. Holmes." Curiosity getting the better of him Sherlock casually inquired "Am I to take from your telephone call that the meeting with your niece did not go as you and Mrs. Houdini had anticipated?"

Harry Houdini acting as if his conversation with Sherlock might be confidential and inadvertently over heard answered "can we go inside where we can talk privately?" Entering the now busy...bustling and noisy eatery Sherlock scanned the collection of tables in front of him each now filled with seated noon hour patrons...then he spotted a still empty table with two chairs near the rear of Balthazar's.

"Over there Mr. Houdini" as Sherlock pointed out his prize...with that the two men carefully worked their way from the entrance though seated customers and waiters taking lunch orders and serving food to the unoccupied table.

After they had both been comfortably seated Sherlock to assure an obviously cautious Mr. Houdini said "I believe with our location whatever news you have to share with me will be safe. Now please relate the details of what took place with your niece when you asked her about her visits to Greenwich Village?"

During the luncheon meal Harry Houdini related the emotional events that had occurred during the previous evening he and his wife had shared with Marie and how he had tried to gently approach the subject and at the same time express his doubts to her.

"And your nieces reaction to your concerns was" Sherlock asked with great curiosity. "All she said to me when I tried to broach the subject with her Mr. Holmes was *No Uncle Harry...if there is any sadness in my life right now it is because of the demands my employer is making on me and the other girls at work. There seems so much to do and not enough time to do it in.*"

"I do not wish to concern you Mr. Houdini...but I believe with her somewhat nonchalant answer your niece appears to have become too ensnared in Miss Taggart's trap so that none of us can be of any real help to her. Our focus will there for have to shift from the one who is trapped to the one who created the trap."

Chapter 35

"I hope you realize the confidential and sensitive nature of the messages I reveal to you each time Miss Hinson. They are never to hinted at or be shared with anyone" here Ashley emphasised not even with Marie's family.

"The trust that has made this possible has been established between you and I and between me and the sprit giving and is fragile and it can be irrevocably broken with just a misplaced word."

Marie noted that with each previous visit to the medium the voice she was used to hearing coming from across a familiar table had sounded...although mysterious yet confident.

This time though there was a slight edge to the mediums voice while delivering the cautionary warning...as if she had received some bad news or had somehow lost her connection to the spirit world.

What Marie did not have any knowledge of was that Ashley had received a visitor earlier...he had not come seeking any spiritual help or message from the beyond but to impart one that came with a warning.

Peter Eastman (the visitor) as Ashley's lawyer had come to pass along the specific counsel he had received earlier in his office from his client.

Peter detailed all the events that had recently happened concerning the medium. He listed all the people involved with any interest in her spiritual affairs he started with "there is my wife Alice."

Ashley stopped Peter for a moment and coldly stated "I have already met her." Pausing to take in this surprising revelation Peter continued..."then there is Mr. Sherlock Holmes...the famous English consulting detective...his friend Mrs. Mary Watson the widow of Dr. John Watson...Mrs. Bess Houdini the wife of the man who could cause you a lot of trouble...Harry Houdini."

When the details had been fully revealed including Harry Houdini's opinion concerning spiritualists...Ashley thought about the information...thinking that none of it had any real impact on her and on her new found career gave Peter a distinct "what does any of this have to do with me" expression.

Peter to impress upon Ashley the seriousness of the situation challenged her indifferent look with "I believe one of your clients you are seeing is named Marie Hinson is that correct? "

The medium affirmed this by nodding yes. Then like a large oak tree that has been chopped almost all the way through and ready to fall Peter delivered the final blow with the words "She is the niece of Harry and Bess Houdini."

Chapter 36

For the next part of Sherlock's and my visit to New York City with Alice and Peter the atmosphere had changed considerably. Although he could have occasionally joined us only Alice, Sherlock and I continued (by day) to take in the sights and destinations this city is famous for.

The three of us saw nothing of Peter in the morning during our normally shared breakfast...and Alice had stopped making excuses for his absence. When Peter started to return home later and from work...he would take the dinner plate that been kept warm in the oven and eat the evening meal in his study.

I had some idea as to when this might have come about...and oddly enough how it might have started with a book Alice had in her collection that I was interested in and had chosen to read while I was staying in New York City.

On entering the Eastman home for the first time I...while taking in the ground floor interior of the house noticed that Alice and Peter had an impressive collection of hard cover books displayed in two large standing book shelves each one situated against the wall on cither side of the ground floor bay window.

When I inquired about the literary collection...Alice had answered "history and fiction...most of the books are mine and they came from my parent's house just after Peter and I had moved. The remaining books belong to Peter and I believe they have to do with the area of law that he practices.

Later when I had finished unpacking my clothes and putting away my toiletries I left my room and returned down stairs to the parlour where I went to each book case in turn and read down the vertical spines of each hardback to see if I recognized any of their authors and also to see if any of Winifred's work had made the Trans Atlantic journey to join this collection.

While I was looking at a book titled "Harvest" written by Mary Augusta Ward Alice came over to where I was and invited me to pick out a book to read while I was visiting...and she stated that if I didn't finish it I could take it back to London with me and send it back by the post when I was finished.

So during my stay the novel titled "Harvest" was my companion on the nights when for the most part on my own and there wasn't any evening event planned. Most times I would read until around 10:00 p.m. hoping to finish a chapter while sometimes momentarily putting the book down to say good night to Sherlock then Alice.

My last duties before retiring for the night were to first turn out the lights still on down stairs and make sure that any ground floor windows still opened to let in the night breeze were now closed then check that both the front and back doors were locked.

Having completed these tasks then carefully I would manage my way through the now darkened house then quietly climb the stairs and go to my bedroom.

Normally by this time the evening silence that filled the house would occasionally be broken by the sound of a neighbors barking dog or by the noise of the occasional passing automobile...but as I got to the top of the stairs through the closed door of Alice's and Peter's bedroom I could hear the sound of two discordant raised and angry voices.

Not wishing to eavesdrop and try to make any sense of the muffled but obviously very heated words coming from behind their door I turned and made my way to my bedroom hoping that with closing my door I could shut out the fury.

As I came into the kitchen the next morning I saw that Alice was already seated at the table...looking worn and showing little or no interest in the food in front of her

Getting a cup and saucer from the cupboard I poured my morning coffee...sat down next to her and waited for Alice to inevitably unburden herself. Like a sudden and unexpected cloudburst Alice started in with "Mary I have to talk to you" as she was taking a breath before continuing Sherlock not entirely sure of what was about to unfold had made his entrance into the kitchen.

Quickly looking at both of us and making an astute assessment of the situation he said "perhaps I should leave Mrs. Eastman and allow you and Mary to continue talking in private." Alice looked up at Sherlock as if she was about to founder in the ocean replied "no Mr Holmes I would like you to stay...some of what I was about to share with Mary you may be able to help me with."

Chapter 37

Sherlock sat in the kitchen chair next to me and opposite to Alice...he studied my cousin's considerably troubled face as if to gather possible clues about her present state...then when he had found the trail he gestured in her direction and in his consulting detective's voice said "please...continue."

Before starting Alice took a drink from her now lukewarm cup of coffee and began to relate to both of us the details she had been made privileged to concerning her husband's rather surprising and unexpected appearance in Greenwich Village.

Before Alice got too far along with her narrative Sherlock momentarily stopped her and asked how she had come to know what she was relating to us. "From a Mrs. Brenda Wright...she and I are volunteers with the American Foundation for the Blind...it's a gathering of about 15 women volunteers who meet each Wednesday afternoon."

"Could this Mrs. Wright be certain that the person she saw that day was in fact your husband?" Sherlock inquired "She was sure because she has met and been introduced to Peter a number of times at various social functions that both he and I have attended."

Alice answered back with certainly "Did she tell you of his final destination?" Sherlock further inquired "Yes and she told me she had seen him push one of the apartment door buzzers at 141 Wooster Street."

When Alice had finished giving the details she had learned Sherlock summed up the narrative with "As the result of your visit to this address Mrs. Eastman we know the identity of only one resident living at that address.

Mr. Eastman for some reason had decided to pay a visit to her. Searching to make a connection Sherlock then asked my cousin "Your husband practices law is that correct? " Alice quickly nodded yes "Do you know what area of law your husband and his law firm may have an interest in?" "Stage and film actors, musician's escape artists and magicians I believe Mr. Holmes" was Alice's answer

Sherlock quickly came to a conclusion to ease a wife's martial suspicions..."With these facts let us assume for the moment that until proven otherwise the visit witnessed by Mrs. Wright may be seen strictly in the professional context of a barrister merely calling on a client.

We do not know what was discussed or what may have transpired. But with the unusual legal and mystical combination of Mr. Eastman and Miss Taggart it would seem that both your husband and the law firm he is employed with may have branched out into a new area of law that now includes the interests of mediums and spiritualists here in New York City.

Chapter 38

From what Mr. Houdini has shared during our many conversations I have come to learn in the entertainment profession or business the run of a show means how many performances it will present to an audience on stage before closing or ending.

Harry Houdini's The Supreme Ruler of Mystery Magical Revue show was about half way through its run when he received word from the manager that the Hippodrome Theater would have to close for a time to undertake much needed renovations.

Upon receiving information that his booking agent had located an available theater Harry Houdini found himself making a day trip from New York City to Weehawken, New Jersey (just across the river) to see if The Atrium (which had been suggested) ...located at 1000 Harbor Boulevard would suite his temporary needs.

In the morning just shortly after he had said goodbye to his wife...telling her that he would be back by supper there was an unexpected knock at the front door of a brownstone located at 278 W 113 Street in Harlem.

Bess Houdini went to answer thinking that it might be her husband returning because he had forgotten something. When she opened the door to her considerable surprise she saw her niece standing at the threshold waiting to enter. Caught unaware by the unexpected visit Bess Houdini with cursory glance of Marie tried to surmise why her niece was not at work but where she was at this moment.

Not quite sure as to how to greet Marie...the best her aunt could muster was "Well come in dear." As her niece entered the house and walked pass her aunt to take off and hang up her coat she asked "Is Uncle Harry at home?"

Now more confused than ever about the nature of this unplanned visit Bess Houdini answered "No he has gone to Weehawken, New Jersey for the day to visit a theater that will house his show while renovations are being carried out on the Hippodrome."

"Is there something I could help you with?" Marie stood in front of her Aunt wanting to desperately tell her the real reason for the visit...but because Ashley the medium had sworn her to a terrible secrecy and that at the same time was demanding more money for her to stay in contact with the spirit of Trevyn James Craddock she couldn't.

Seeing that her niece was troubled while trying to give an answer to a simple question Bess Houdini offered her the hospitality of inviting Marie to stay and share the lunch she until now was up to now going to eat on her own.

While sharing the noon time meal of tomato rice soup and toast Bess Houdini would occasionally look up at Marie and try to speculate what was troubling her. After a series of probing questions that were resulting in one syllable answers Bess Houdini quietly got up from the table and left the kitchen for a moment.

When she returned she took Marie's right hand...opened it and placed what she that thought would be enough money to solve Marie's apparent problem. As she closed Marie's hand her niece looked up and said "thank you Aunt Bess."

As Bees Houdini was setting the table for supper she heard her husband come through the front door of their residence. "I'm home Bess" she heard him cheerily announce as the door was being closed...she brightly returned "I'm in the kitchen."

When harry Houdini entered the kitchen as had been a comfortable habit for their married life each shared the events that had taken place in their respective day.

"I think the Atrium will suit the needs of the show during the renovations. Granted it's smaller than the Hippodrome but if we schedule afternoon matinees for Mondays Wednesdays and Fridays we shouldn't see too big a drop in attendance...and how was your day?"

"Marie came by unexpectedly this afternoon." Here Bess Houdini paused for a moment then continued "I knew there something wrong as soon as I opened the door to let her in." Sounding very much like a concerned uncle that Harry Houdini was he asked "Did she say what?" then as an acknowledgement of his wife's skills...did you find out what?"

"I tried as gently and as unobtrusively as I could during lunch to find out what was bothering her...but all I received were one word answers. I'm sorry Harry but I didn't want to push so in the end all I could think was that she was having money problems so I gave her some cash to try and help her."

"You did what you thought was right Bess"...mildly puzzled by his wife's statement Harry Houdini shook his head from side to side then continued "but from what I know of her employment and employer our Marie earns a good wage and even with her rent and other monthly expenses she should have some money set aside for a rainy day."

Not sure that she was entirely following her husband's line of reasoning...almost in despair Bess Houdini asked "what are we going to do Harry?" Harry Houdini reached across the table and gently laid his hands on his wife's while looking into her eyes to assure her that everything was about to get better he said "we are going to find an umbrella for Marie."

Chapter 39

Marie's visits to Greenwich Village had started in the spring time...when all was warm and fine the leaves on the trees were a bright green and all the flower boxes along the walk were full of blooms of varied colors.

What had been dark gloomy days after leaving the admitting ward of the New York Methodist Hospital having asked about her fiancé...and given a cold and heartless reception now as she was going to her appointment to see the medium She felt a spring time within her for the first time...knowing that although she might not hear Trevyns voice but would hear (through the medium) of what he thought...felt and wanted to say to her.

As the gentle spring time weather became an increasingly hot and humid summer Marie was not certain if she could make the trip as it was both physically as well as an emotionally draining.

But like someone parched and lost in a vast and featureless desert looking for any oasis Marie kept coming back to 141 Wooster Street to collect the few drops of relief Ashley (for a price) was willing to part with.

Now it was autumn...for Marie it was not to be an autumn of vibrant colors...familiar sounds and smells we remember as children ...or anticipate and enjoy as adults...of brief warm and almost summer like days...watching leaves on trees magically change from verdant green to the bright reds oranges and yellows of the season...of listening to the dry swishing and crunching sound feet make while walking through the piles of ones that have already fallen...of sweet-smelling late picked crisp to the bite apples and pumpkins of all shapes and sizes waiting in fields to be taken away and transformed for one night into Halloween candle lit jack o lanterns or just out of the oven warm and delicious aromatic holiday pies.

For her it was to be an autumn of low overcast dull lead grey colored skies...for her an autumn filled with endless days of cold hard rain falling as a torrential down pour one minute determined to wash away the very last remnants of summer then gradually slowing down to a few sparse and intermittent drops...each small globule of icy water reflected in...and finally ending its downward journey in irregular shaped puddles they create.

Chapter 40

In all the years I have known and written about Sherlock I have always acknowledged him as someone methodical in his way...with plans thought out well ahead before beginning any undertaking and rarely if ever giving into spontaneity. So I was surprised when at breakfast one morning he asked Alice if just he and I spend the day together touring the sites of this great city.

Both Alice and I were somewhat curious as to where and what Sherlock had in mind. I could tell that he had more in mind than what he was casually suggesting when he announced "I was thinking Mary that you and I should spend the day at the American Museum of Natural History. Which I believe is located at Central Park West and 79th street."

Trying to follow his lead I nodded my head in agreement. And almost as if to convince Alice that this outing was nothing more than two close friends spending the day together Sherlock finished with "It should be interesting to compare the American Museum of Natural History in New York to the British Museum in London."

-

On our taxicab ride from the Eastman's into down town New York my curiosity got the better of me and I found myself asked my travelling companion why he had chosen Central Park West and 79th street.

"It's not so much the location Mary...but rather that we can talk in private" Sherlock started. "I received another phone call from Mr. Houdini and he wants this business with his niece and the medium brought to an end."

"Although I do not believe that anything Mrs. Eastman might be party to...if we were to discuss this with her would be intentionally passed along to Mr. Eastman it is best that for her sake as well as for ours she be excluded from the conversation we are about to have. Sometimes it is the most innocent and innocuous remarks made in general conversation that can cause the most damage."

When we entered the museum we didn't have any itinerary planned as to what we would see first then go onto next...rather we meandered past exhibits and in and out of display halls all time trying to come up with a plan to rescue Marie...the Houdini's niece from the medium and at the same time possibly convince the medium Miss Taggart to accompany Sherlock and me back to London.

For most of the time we had the museum to ourselves and could talk fairly openly...however as we were heading to the last feature of the museum "the fossil hall" containing the preserved remains of ancient reptiles the direction of our visit took an unexpected change in direction.

 As we had done before we entered the hall solely with the intention of continuing our conversation and not really paying any sort of attention to our surroundings...when to my surprise I saw a young lady coming towards us with the obvious intention of quickly leaving. It was as she got closer I realized who it was and began to wonder why she was here.

There was that moment of recognition that passed between Ashley and me each of us then expecting the other to change direction and avoid any contact.

But I chose not and so did she...when we were as close as was necessary...Ashley not wanting to lose the momentary advantage said in an extremely sarcastic tone of voice "Mrs Watson...what a totally unpleasant surprise...made more so by seeing you here again."

Continuing in this vein Ashley after indifferently sizing up Sherlock said to him with equal sarcasm "and you must be the famous consulting detective Sherlock Holmes."

Sherlock totally unfazed by this verbal assault returned "You must be Miss Ashley Laurinda Taggart" pausing for a second he continued "the medium who I am given to understand conducts her business in an apartment located in Greenwich Village."

"This chance meeting is interesting because Mrs. Watson and I have just been discussing you at length and trying to come up with a plan for you to release Miss Hinson from her spiritual contract and accompany us back to London to face the justice you have so skillfully eluded."

Up until now Ashley had been mildly indifferent as to what Sherlock and I were saying to her...but with Sherlock's stated plan she gave him a look that bordered on pure hatred defensively she shot back "you may have some authority as a consulting detective in London Mr. Holmes.

This may come (she sarcastically added) from your collaboration with the Metropolitan Police in arresting persons such as myself.

But as things stand right you have no authority here in this city and in this country and cannot interfere with anyone who comes to me seeking help and comfort or even force me to return to England. You and Mrs. Watson to me are nothing more than two very troublesome and meddlesome tourists."

Not giving either Sherlock or myself a chance to challenge her declaration...without so much as saying goodbye she abruptly started to walk away from us and make her way towards the exit.

At no more than 20 paces from where we were left standing the medium stopped as if she had a question to ask. Not sure what was to happen next I watched as she slowly turned back to us ...coldly observed Sherlock and I as a hunter would perceive its prey...then in a tone that we both fully understood said "Good day and enjoy your visit to the museum. By the way give my regards to the Houdini's when you see then next...and have a safe and problem free voyage home on The Majestic"

Chapter 41

From further conversations with Mr. Houdini I was starting to understand his world and the world his niece found herself in. Spiritualism (he told me) has been the cause of much discussion between men of science, men of magic, and believers in the "Spirit World."

Countless investigations, wise and otherwise, have been held in most of the countries of the globe. Many of them have been made by fair-minded, unbiased men; men who delved deep into the unknown with a clear conscience and whether successful or not were willing to give the world the result of their probing.

Many who are not afraid to admit that their experience was not sufficient to cope with the medium's skill and years of training and that they had been fooled. But there have been other so-called investigators who have attended séances wishing to be fooled and as "the wish is father of the thought" they have been misled.

What these investigators *see* done and what they *think* they see done are in reality two entirely different things and by the time they start to write their experiences there are usually complications.

I rarely believe a full hundred per cent the explanations I hear or read. It is to be said to the credit of the investigators that they do not deliberately make misstatements but the nature of the brain is such that it is almost impossible to avoid malobservation and these mal-observations are the curse of investigation.

Investigations under conditions favorable to the medium cannot be termed "investigations." They are nothing more than a demonstration of the medium's power to divert the attention, carrying it at will to any place they wish and numbing the subconscious mind.

Under such conditions they are not only able to delude the innocent and simple-minded but also men whose accomplishments have proven their intellects to be above the average.

When a medium is subjected to conditions which are, to say the least, disconcerting, and the usual effects are not obtained, almost invariably the claim is made that there are antagonistic waves and that the "auras" are bad, and if, as often happens, the result is an unqualified expose and the medium's fall from power the followers of Spiritualism usually put forth a statement saying the medium overstepped the bounds in trying to give results and resorted to trickery, but that the majority of previous séances were genuine .

Perhaps his ideas on the subject of how to conduct an investigation were wrong; he was fully convinced, however, that the only way to conduct a successful one is to get the committee together previous to the séance, discuss the expected manifestations, and formulate some plan for concerted action and if possible assign each member some specific part. These parts should be rehearsed and then when the séance is held there is a much greater possibility of the committee being able to judge intelligently.

But when scientists report some feat of legerdemain as being abnormal simply because they cannot detect the deception, he thought it is time to add to each investigating committee a successful and reputable professional mystifier, and might add that all mediums hate to have a magician attend a séance. The next séance the medium conducted would in fact not be attended by a magician but from an unknown relative of the deceased person she was using to keep Marie coming back.

Chapter 42

Ashley Laurinda Taggart had been born into and had grown up in a world where she had quickly learned to be a survivor. She had learned to deal with the many unexpected the twists and turns that life had presented to her. But her chance encounter with Sherlock and me at the museum...despite her emboldened attitude towards us had left her surprisingly shaken and uncertain.

As she was putting the key into the door of her apartment to open it and enter she was beginning to reflect that it might be time to move to a city where she would be unknown and could make a fresh start in her new career. After removing her hat and coat she went into the galley kitchen to brew a cup of calming camomile tea then sit down and take stock of the present situation.

While seated at her table blowing over the lip of the cup to cool its contents and also the thoughts in her mind the telephone started to ring. Uncertain as to who would be calling...Ashley put the cup down...brought the ringing telephone to where she could reach it...picked up the receiver and cautiously said into it "Hello?"

The only characteristic of the voice she heard in the receiver that she could recognize was of an older woman...and that the woman was speaking with an accent that Ashley could not immediately place. There was an awkward moment of silence then the older female caller asked "is this the person who placed an advertisement in the paper about searching for peace of mind?"

The newspaper advertisement that had the started the present long chain of events briefly flashed in front of Ashley's eyes when she heard herself say "yes it is" Suddenly being presented with a possible way out of an increasingly difficult situation the medium in a very businesslike tone of voice asked "may I ask who is speaking...and how may I be of assistance?"

There was a pause as if Ashley's immediate answer had caught the caller off guard then... "My name is Anwyn Crunn. I have travelled from Penrhyn Bay a small town on the north coast of Wales to New York City. I have only recently come to learn about the unfortunate death of my nephew Trevyn James Craddock in this city and I wish some how to make contact to speak with him and say goodbye.

Realizing that she was probably going to eventually lose her grasp on Marie as a client due to the revealed efforts of Sherlock and I Ashley quickly responded "Miss Crunn where are you staying while you are visiting?" "The Chelsea Mews Guest House 344 W 15th Street" the caller responded.

The unexpected call finished with the medium writing down a contact number and giving her new client directions as to how to arrive at apartment 4d 141 Wooster Street. As with previous clients there were the explicit instructions that the medium would see the aunt of the deceased nephew at this time and day next week.

Hanging up the telephone Ashley was elated that she had one last person to take advantage of and that this person would help her earn enough money to shortly say goodbye to Greenwich Village.

Taking one more sip of the now tepid beverage she got up and went to where she kept her files on all the clients she had performed "spiritual readings" for. Witnessing the collection any consulting detective would have been impressed with as to how much detailed information each file contained and the amount of work each of her confederates had put into making Ashley seem to be a credible spiritual medium.

Taking one particular file back to the table...Ashley sat down opened it up and started looking through it and rereading familiar names and facts in the hope of getting to know about this new Welsh aunt.

Chapter 43

The front entrance to 141 Wooster Street in Greenwich Village most mornings and afternoons had been taken on the appearance of a railway station platform with a variety of people...not unlike passengers who after pushing the door buzzer for apartment 4d could be seen standing and waiting patiently for the medium to come down the stairs to escort them up to her parlour and to her spirit world.

At first it had been novelty and something of a game the long term residents of Greenwich Village had played trying to guess something of the waiting person's personality and what had brought them to seek out Ashley's help. But now any one passing by the entrance gave the person standing there no more than a passing glance.

Anwyn Crunn was no different; she looked and dressed like any woman of her age and stature in New York City and there for was not really noticed. The only difference that would have set her apart from any one else was her Penrhyn Bay small town on the north coast of Wales accent.

Having not heard or witnessed anything in response to her first attempt at pushing the door buzzer for apartment 4d Anwyn first checked the note she had written the details of the appointment on...then pushed the door buzzer again.

This time hearing the sounds of women's shoes lightly descending the stairs...the Welsh aunt took in a breath and prepared to meet Ashley. It seemed like an eternity then the door opened in and both the medium and the one seeking her help stood and briefly, each for their own personal reasons quickly assessed each other.

As Ashley welcomed her guest in and asked her to follow her up the stairs she realized she was not on proceeding on firm ground. First the file she had been examining had made no reference to any Welsh aunt and that when she had first looked at the woman now following her up the stairs there had been the briefest flash of recognition.

Taking the aunts coat Ashley directed her to sit in the chair the previous client had come to know. Not sure about the doubt that was starting to cloud her mind that she wanted to continue the medium said "I will make a pot of tea to relax us both."

While the kettle was starting to boil and as she was getting the tea ready Ashley to push away any misgivings bravely started to ask what she hoped would be interpreted as nothing more than innocent questions. With each correct answer about Trevyn from the aunt Ashley's doubts about the older woman now seated at the table started to diminish.

When the last cup of tea had been poured into both cups...Ashley dispelling any lingering doubts in the same manner that you would with brushing away remaining cobwebs in a corner of the room said "Shall we begin?"

As the procedure with Marie Hinson had been described to me earlier it was the same for Anwyn. The appearance of successful scrying (reading) again depended on the created mood and atmosphere. Ashley did not want to appear to force herself into a reading session.

The medium found crystal ball gazing was easiest in a quiet, dimly lit room. She had lit a couple of candles...when asked why she explained the reflections of the flames help to summon images.

The important thing the medium remembered was to create an atmosphere for the person sitting in front of her. After all if someone walked in unexpectedly...not that they would be allowed to, they should instantly be aware that something significant is taking place."

When Ashley removed the white silk handkerchief...Anwyn for the first time looked into the same crystal ball that Marie had gazed upon for so many times. Ashley relaxed in her chair then laid her hands gently on the ball...giving the appearance that somehow she was energizing it and at the same time strengthening it with some psychic rapport.

Holding the crystal ball carefully in her hands with eyes now closed Ashley appeared to be thinking about the purpose of the visit when in fact she was really assessing what the aunt wanted to know about her nephew.

Her face changed to one of absolute concentration while in her mind she went through all the information in one particular file...but to the person sitting in front of her it appeared as if to Ashley was trying to visualize the question Anwyn had travelled all this way to ask.

The medium slowly moved her hands away from the crystal ball...and appeared to stare deeply into the center of it. Her voice from across the table....barely an audible whisper said "I can see a mist or smoke starting to form in the crystal...ask what you came here for."

The aunt took a moment to think about what she wanted to ask...she wanted to ask questions that came with definitive answers...she wanted the memory of her nephew and all that knew him finally put to rest. When Anwyn had finished...Ashley a little louder announced "the mist grows and fills the ball, I can visualise it gradually clearing to reveal images within the crystal."

"The images or answers that appear to see might not be what you expected. That's OK, don't fight them. Your subconscious mind knows what information you need. Just let the images flow, changing and taking you wherever they choose to go. Don't try to rationalise now, time for that later."

For about the next twenty minutes Ashley, methodically one by one from memory accurately answered all of the concerned aunt's questions.

When she had exhausted the contents of the file she mysteriously stated "Once the crystal ball has shown you all the images you need and you have shared them, they will begin to fade. I must now reverse the process I used at the beginning. The mists are coming back and covering the images, they have now receded and the crystal ball is returning to its natural state."

The medium thinking that her performance had been both convincing and believable placed the white silk handkerchief back over the crystal ball to indicate the reading was done. She rose from the table knowing that her guest would too.

Somewhere between the guest putting her coat on and being escorted to the front door the agreed upon fee for services rendered would be exchanged. Feeling confident Ashley as she was putting the money into one her dress pockets said "I'm glad I could be of help to you and your nephew Miss Crunn...are you staying in New York for a while or are you thinking of going home?"

Anwyn Crunn (a distant aunt of Trevyn James Craddock) from Penrhyn Bay a small town on the north Wales coast, in Conwy county borough, within the parish or community of Llandudno, and part of the *ecclesiastical* parish of Llanrhos. Penrhyn Bay is a prosperous village with a cluster of local shops; a pub and a parish church smiled and replied "no I have completed what I had set out to while I was here. There is however one question you did not answer Miss Taggart wasn't Trevyn keeping company with a young lady named Marie Hinson who I believe is the niece of the Houdini's?" Wasn't Miss Hinson also consulting with you to try and contact him?

Chapter 44

Hearing those words Ashley suddenly shocked reacted as if she had heard and witnessed some horrible and terrible automobile accident.

At that moment the blood seemed to drain from her hands and feet and she suddenly felt cold and terrified. Quickly regaining her composure she clinically analyzed the person standing in front of her who had just said them...then like a rattlesnake lunging to attack she blurted out the words "Mary Watson!"

"Yes it is me" I said as I removed my wig to reveal my true hair color. Missing her target she attacked again by asking "how did you come to know...and who have you been in contact with?" When she realized I wasn't going to divulge any information her voice took on a more petulant tone

"What are your plans for me then?" then in a slightly more combative voice "and do you really think you can carry them out?"

Watching her trying to get around me and make her escape out the door...I pointed to the chair she had been occupying and strongly instructed her to go back there to sit and wait.

Seeing her seated again cautiously I made my way to the door...opened just enough and said in a voice loud enough to be heard at the entrance "Constable...you may come up now and make your arrest. It was only a short time later when another police constable was seen entering the law firm of Archer & Greiner P.C. (personal and confidential)....to arrest the co conspirator to this crime of spiritual fraud

---

There was only one last detail to be attended to before this matter could be brought to a final close and then Sherlock and I could start to think about returning home. After making a telephone call to a still concerned uncle we found ourselves at a brownstone located at 278 W 113 Street in Harlem waiting to be invited in.

"Mr. Houdini before leaving New York City Mrs. Watson and I have come to bring you and Mrs Houdini some much needed good news." Looking relieved Harry Houdini gestured for us to sit. Then getting up and taking a couple of steps towards the kitchen he called "Bess...Mr. Holmes and Mrs. Watson are here and they have news they want to share with us."

When Bess Houdini joined us while controlling a satisfied smile that was starting to play on his face Sherlock related to the couple "its concerning your niece Miss Hinson...she will no longer have any need to travel to Wooster Street in Greenwich Village.

She will also no longer need the services of the medium she has been seeing" As another look of relief came over Harry and Bess Houdini's face Bess Houdini with concern asked "have you taken care of the medium then Mr. Holmes?"

Here Sherlock showed a rare display of pride in what I had just accomplished..."not me Mrs. Houdini...but rather Mrs. Watson in the convincing guise and Welsh accent of a long lost aunt of Trevyn James Craddock that the medium thought she could include in the company of your niece and her deceased young gentleman."

Chapter 45

With all changes that had taken place and events that had happened during our stay Sherlock and I were looking forward to a final enjoyable evening in New York City with Alice seeing Harry Houdini and his wife perform (at their invitation) one last time before boarding our ship the next morning for our return voyage home to England.

Ever the showman Harry Houdini made his entrance onto the large stage basking in the spot lights and sound of the thunderous applause..."And for my final act this evening I would like to perform an illusion for you I call it the Davenport Cabinet act.

Normally I would have my wife enter then disappear but for a change I will call for someone from the audience...as we are honoured again to have among us tonight at the Hippodrome theater a very famous gentleman from England who because of his reputation does not need an introduction...I would like to call on Mr. Sherlock Holmes to please come to the stage."

As Sherlock got up and made his way past me, Alice and the other members of the seated audience to the carpeted aisle he was greeted with a standing ovation...it continued as he went down the aisle to the stairs the lead to the stage. As he made his way up the short flight of stairs to the broad spot lit stage the applause died down. Harry Houdini walked towards Sherlock his right hand extended in greeting. While giving Sherlock a very firm hand shake he stated "Mr. Holmes it is a pleasure it is to have you with us again at the Hippodrome tonight" then so only Sherlock could hear "and thank you for your help" "The pleasure is mine Mr. Houdini" Sherlock returned. Escorting Sherlock to center stage Harry Houdini began his presentation.

"Now before I begin could you please examine the cabinet to verify that it is an ordinary piece of furniture and nothing more?" Sherlock opened the door…closely inspected the interior…soundly rapped with the knuckles of his right hand the four interior walls…then stamped on the floor of the cabinet with his right shoe to see if he could detect a false floor.

When he was satisfied with his interior inspection he walked around the outside of the closet…again soundly tapping the four walls. "If you are satisfied could I have you enter the cabinet please after which I will close the door."

With Sherlock inside and the door now closed I expected some sort of curtain would be drawn up in front cloaking how the person inside made their escape. To my amazement there was to be no curtain… Harry Houdini tapped on the four outside walls much as Sherlock had done previously then with great showmanship announced "Ladies and Gentlemen when I count to three the cabinet will come apart and Mr. Holmes will have vanished."

Dramatically pointing his right hand at the cabinet he gestured and counted "One…Two…Three" with that the cabinet noisily collapsed into six pieces onto the stage in much in the same manner as a house of cards would if sharply blown on and with that Sherlock for all intensive purposes had disappeared.

Then on cue one of the spot lights was directed away from the stage up to an unoccupied seat located on the on the far right side of the second balcony. Confident the illusion had worked and that Sherlock would shortly appear Harry Houdini announced to the audience "ladies and gentlemen I give you Mr. Sherlock Holmes." There was an awkward pause when he didn't appear …thinking that maybe Sherlock may have had gotten temporarily lost in route from the stage to the now lit seat….Harry Houdini a little less confidently announced again "I give you Mr. Sherlock Holmes."

When he failed to materialize the spot light was directed back to the stage and people in the audience started to comment among themselves that if the failure to produce Sherlock had been intended to build anticipation for the act…then certainly the bounds of showmanship and good taste had been crossed.

While Harry Houdini was making attempts to apologize for the failed illusion I was not sure if Sherlock's disappearance was the result of the illusion or if he had suffered some unplanned misfortune so I made my way to the stage to confront Mr. Houdini to find out what he knew. On the way there I overheard comments from the audience I was passing that were variations of "where could he have gone to?"

Making my way up and onto the stage I purposely proceeded in Harry Houdini's direction and confronted him on Sherlock's failure to reappear. He looked a little sheepish at my direct line of questioning because it turned out he already had the answer.

Calming my anxiety he asked me if we could go back into the wings to talk...when the last of the stage hands had gone from the stage area after removing the magic and illusion props from the performance he said "I apologize Mrs. Watson for Mr. Holmes unplanned and somewhat mysterious exit but this" here he handed me an envelope "may explain why."

When he had left me to return to his dressing room I with some trepidation and a growing nameless fear opened the envelope in my hand....I pulled out a single sheet of writing paper...unfolded it and started reading in Sherlock's own handwriting the words "Dear Mary..."

The next morning after saying a sad and final tearful good bye to my cousin Alice...with the book "Harvest" I had borrowed from her in hand I turned and made my way into the waiting taxicab that would take me back into the city to arrive at the New York Passenger Ship Terminal and White Star Line pier 94 then board the Majestic for the crossing back to Southampton.

As I was waiting my turn along with the other assembled travellers to go onto the waiting ship the Majestic's boarding officer first examined my ticket then the passenger manifest.

He looked puzzled for a moment then curiously asked "Weren't you travelling with a gentleman Mrs. Watson?...a Mr. Holmes I believe"...before answering the question I remembered that in his final hand written note Sherlock had instructed me that I was not to let anyone know where he was going or what his future plans were to be.

Composing myself I convincingly answered the question by saying "Mr. Holmes has decided to stay on in New York City for a time to study escape artistry with an expert and will be crossing the Atlantic at a later date and time."

When we least expected the curtain as had been explained was quickly raised up and over his head...with that action two things took place...the curtain no longer being held quickly and dramatically fell and landed on to the stage and there to our surprise was Mrs. Houdini (unbound) standing on top of the crate in her husband's place.

Epilogue

In the early 1900's while performing on the vaudeville circuit, Houdini worked with a couple named Keaton. Their young son Joseph was intrigued by Houdini's magic, and Houdini was quite taken with the boy. Houdini nicknamed him "Buster", and the name stuck, explaining how Buster Keaton, the famous film comedian got his name.

Sherlock Holmes and The Escape Artist notes:

This story is the fourth Sherlock Holmes story I have written. Unlike the previous story... Sherlock Holmes and The Mystery Writer this story uses a mixture of real (alive at the time the story is set characters and people) and fictional characters. The real people in the story are of course Harry Houdini (well known escape artist...illusionist and spiritual debunker) his wife Bess Houdini and their niece Marie Hinson...the daughter of Bess Houdini's sister. As well Stan and Eileen Moore (foster parents) and Elizabeth (my Aunt Bessie) Williams the sister of Eileen Moore.

The fictional people who are also included in the story...are as always Sherlock Holmes and Mary Watson...Mary again being the narrator of the story I introduce the reader to Mary's American Cousin Alice Eastman and her husband Peter Eastman...an invitation to visit from the Eastman's to Mary being the basis of the story.

And I bring back my favorite villain Ashley Taggart (based on my niece) from London to New York City. In the last story she was a small time criminal this time she is involved in a new and more profitable line of criminal activity to challenge Sherlock and Mary one last time.

I connect the real characters in the story to the fictional characters in the story with a romantic link between Marie Hinson to the fictional character of Trevyn James Craddock a young man from St. David's Wales that she meets at an afternoon matinee of her uncle's show.

Sherlock Holmes and The Escape Artist is as much a story as well as a travelogue of New York City in 1922. I try to share in words what my characters see...hear and experience with the reader so they can experience what life was like then. Therefore all the places, locations and events the characters visit or are involved with in the story have been researched are accurate and existed at that time.

As with Sherlock Holmes and The Mystery Writer...Sherlock Holmes and The Escape Artist is recorded and chronicled by Mary Watson (from her perspective) and is for the most part is based around situations and events that happened in her life. This is my fourth book in my Sherlock Holmes collection and the second in what I consider being the Mary Watson collection.

What happens next...well the last paragraph before the epilogue gives the reader a possible hint.

Enjoy

Dedications

To my editor Jayson L. and Brenda W. for doing a great job

To all the restaurants and fast food locations here in Brantford Ontario that provided a great place to write...good food...good coffee a Wi-Fi connection (for on the go research) and an A/C plug in...Many thanks from Mary Watson...and all the characters...both real and fictional in the story and myself...for making this story possible.

Fred

Also from Fred Thursfield

Sherlock Holmes and The Discarded Cigarette

London 1895. A well known author, a theoretical invention made real, and the importance of a sometimes overlooked clue challenge Holmes and Watson to prevent the perfect crime.

Also from Fred Thursfield

Sherlock Holmes and The Terrible Secret

It is the start of the First World War. Sherlock Holmes is coaxed out of a short lived retirement to track down an exotic dancer to retrieve a secret accidentally given to her by a young patent clerk before it falls into the hands of a hostile government. As much a detective story as a brief history of the causes, reasons and the long term futility of a long forgotten war.

Also from Fred Thursfield

Sherlock Holmes and The Mystery Writer

Gravesend 1920. A famous mystery writer, while searching through the remains of a damaged church looking for story ideas, happens upon a document that was never meant to be found or read. Any knowledge of its contents could change the terms of the treaty that ended the First World War. There is also a change in the hand that writes and records the cases of Sherlock Holmes.

Save Undershaw

MX Publishing is proud to support the campaign to save and restore Sir Arthur Conan Doyle's former home. Undershaw is where he brought Sherlock Holmes back to life, and should be preserved for future generations of Holmes fans.

Save Undershaw   www.saveundershaw.com

Facebook   www.facebook.com/saveundershaw

You can read more about Sir Arthur Conan Doyle and Undershaw in Alistair Duncan's book (share of royalties to the Undershaw Preservation Trust) – An Entirely New Country and in the amazing compilation Sherlock's Home – The Empty House (all royalties to the Trust).

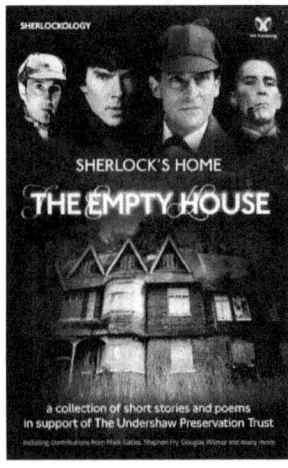